# Buffy

## the Vampire Slayer™

SEASON EIGHT VOLUME 7

# TWILIGHT

Script BRAD MELTZER

Pencils GEORGES JEANTY

Inks ANDY OWENS

Colors MICHELLE MADSEN

Letters RICHARD STARKINGS & COMICRAFT'S JIMMY BETANCOURT

Cover Artist JO CHEN

"Turbulence" and "Goddesses and Monsters"
Script JOSS WHEDON

"Goddesses and Monsters"
Pencils KARL MOLINE

Executive Producer JOSS WHEDON

Dark Horse Books®

President & Publisher MIKE RICHARDSON

Editor SCOTT ALLIE

Associate Editor SIERRA HAHN

Assistant Editors FREDDYE LINS & BRENDAN WRIGHT

Collection Designer TONY ONG

This story takes place after the end of the
television series *Buffy the Vampire Slayer,*
created by Joss Whedon.

Special thanks to Debbie Olshan at Twentieth Century Fox, Natalie Farrell, and Nicki Maron.





*This volume reprints the comic-book series* Buffy the Vampire Slayer *Season Eight #31–#35, and* Willow: Goddesses and Monsters *from Dark Horse Comics.*

Published by
Dark Horse Books
A division of
Dark Horse Comics, Inc.
10956 SE Main Street
Milwaukie, OR 97222

darkhorse.com

To find a comics shop in your area,
call the Comic Shop Locator Service toll-free at (888) 266-4226.

First edition: October 2010
ISBN 978-1-59582-558-2

1 3 5 7 9 10 8 6 4 2
Printed at Interglobe Printing, Inc., Beauceville, QC, Canada

# TURBULENCE

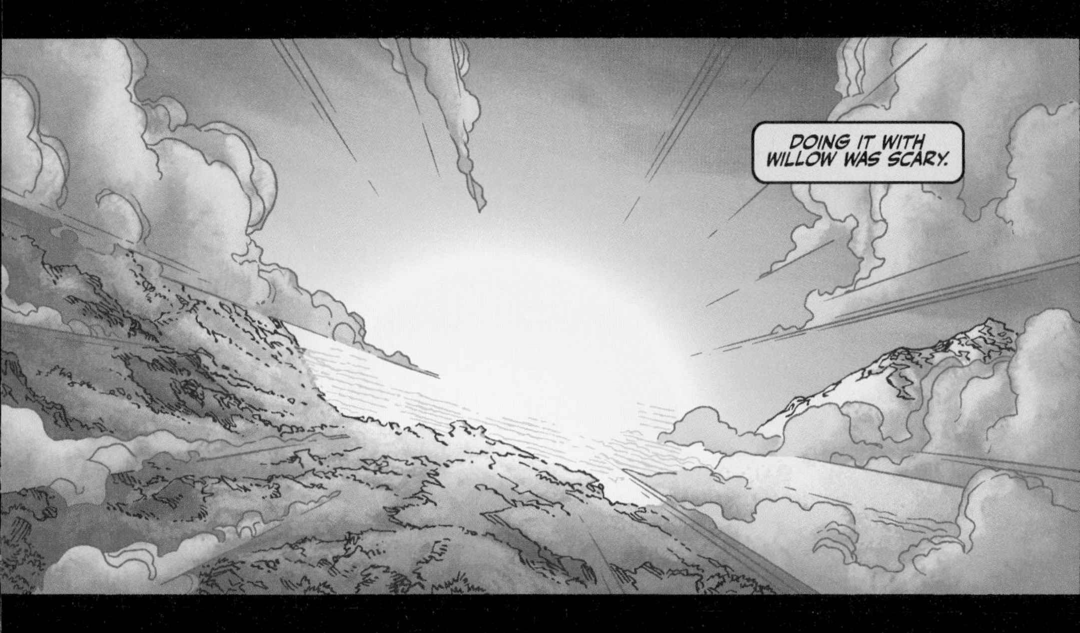
DOING IT WITH WILLOW WAS SCARY.

DOING IT ALONE...
WEIRD.
AND SCARY.

I FEEL STRONGER.

AND I'M WAY BETTER AT LANDING.

BUT WHY?
WHY NOW?
WHY DOES IT FEEL SO NATURAL...

AND WHY DO I STILL WANT TO HIDE IT?

WE'LL GO, OF COURSE.

AS SOON AS WE CAN DEAL WITH THE THREE GIANT RAMPAGING GODDESSES, SEE TO OUR WOUNDED AND FIGURE OUT WHAT TO DO WITH *THEIR* WOUNDED...AND GET OUR POWERS BACK... SOMEHOW...
OZ, I'M SO SORRY.

WE'LL BE ALL RIGHT. BAY'S GONNA BE FINE, AND EVERYONE KNEW WHAT--
WE BROUGHT WAR TO A PLACE OF PEACE.
IT'S TIBET, WILL. YOU'RE NOT THE FIRST.
YOU ALWAYS KNOW WHAT TO SAY, WHEN YOU BOTHER TO TALK.
ANY THOUGHTS ON HOW TO GET MY MAGIC BACK REAL FAST?

WILLOW!
MAN...
YOU DON'T KID AROUND.
I DIDN'T DO THAT.
NO...
IT WAS...LIKE AN AFTERSHOCK. FALLOUT FROM SOME CATACLYSMIC MYSTICAL EVENT.
YOU KNOW WHAT IT WAS?
NO...
IT HASN'T HAPPENED YET.

WILL, SIX OF OUR WICCANS JUST KEELED OVER AND *HEY* MAGIC LOOK AT YOU.
TWO OF THEM BARFED.

A TEMPORAL RIPPLE. FROM SOMETHING POWERFUL AND COMING SOON. SLAYERS?
NO CHANGE. BUT N
WE HAVE A SHOT
GETTING THE *ANDRE*
*SISTERS OF DEAT*
OFF OF OZ'S LAWN
ANDREW HA
SISTERS?

FEMALE TRIO. DESTINY'S CHILD, SHONEN KNIFE... DIXIE CHICKS!
YOU KNOW, YO
*CAN* JUST SAY
THE THING
YOU MEAN.

THE GIRLS SHOULD BE FINE. SEE IF THEY CAN IDENTIFY THE EVENT. I'LL WORK ON THE GODDESSES.
IF I CAN GET THEM BACK UNDERGROUND, MAYBE EVERYONE WILL BE BACK TO FULL POWER.
"PRETTY IMPRESSIVE, RIGHT?"

I'M LIKE GENERAL CUSTER WITH LONG BLOND HAIR.
GENERAL CUSTER *HAD* LONG BLOND HAIR.
SO WE *ARE* DUMBER.

BUFFY.

FOUGHT BRUTAL MPAIGN.
NOBODY WON, BUT NOBODY DOES. I SAW INTELLIGENCE, COURAGE, AND COMPASSION. YOU'RE TREATING THE ENEMY'S WOUNDED.

I'M PROUD OF YOU.

DID THEY GIVE YOU THE *MOST* MORPHINE?
PLUS A FEW SHOTS OF JACK, BUT I THINK I'M GOOD TO DRIVE.

SLEEP, DRUNKIE.
SIR, YES SIR.

"FOR A WHILE, THEY'LL BE LOST."
SO MUCH DESTRUCTION, SO MANY FALLEN...
FACTOR IN THE CONFUSION SPELL MY OWN WICCANS TOSSED INTO THE FIELD AND IT WILL BE HOURS BEFORE YOU ARE MISSED.
DAYS BEFORE YOU'RE SOUGHT.
BUT WHEN BUFFY REALIZES WHAT SHE'S MISSING... SUCH POWERFUL ELEMENTS IN HER MAKEUP...
HER TRUST...
HER GUILT...
AND YOUR NAME WILL COME BACK TO ME...

THINGS WILL START TO HAPPEN VERY QUICKLY.
THE TRUTH. AT LONG LAST, THE MANIFEST TRUTH. BUFFY WILL FINALLY SEE...

"...IF SHE IS ABLE TO SEE AT ALL."

COME ON! CAN'T YOU GET BETTER RECEPTION?

MAYBE IT'S THE MOUNTAINS.
WE STILL HAVE A LOT OF PEOPLE UNACCOUNTED FOR.
A BUNCH OF THEM SCATTERED INTO THE WOODS. IT'LL TAKE THEM A WHILE TO CIRCLE BACK.

WE SHOULD SEND OUT A...

...OR WAIT. WE CAN WAIT. THEY'LL SHOW.

PUNT
SO, OW...
I'M BACK TO BEING SORCERESS SUPREME, BUT THESE GALS ARE STILL WAY OUT OF MY LEAGUE.
IF THEY REACH A POPULATED AREA...

NO.
NO MORE.

DAAHH! WHAT AM I, A HACKY SACK?

ARE YOU A WITCH?

I'M A VAMPIRE SLAYER.
WHAT'S THAT?
JUST LIKE IT SOUNDS

THEY SAID IF WE WERE CAPTURED, YOU'D...DO THINGS TO US. THAT YOU ALL HAVE MAGIC POWERS.
IF WE STILL DID, WE WOULD HAVE HEALED YOU BY NOW.

ARE YOU IN LOVE?

I THINK MAYBE WE SHOULD TAKE IT SLOW...
JENNA ABRAMS. SHE HAS NO IDEA.
I SHOULDA SAID SOMETHING AT THE DANCE, BUT...

WHAT WAS I AFRAID OF? WHAT COULD BE...
WHAT WOULD BE WORSE THAN...

WE'RE GONNA NEED THAT BED.
HOW ABOUT YOU? HAD US WORRIED.
I'M...
I'M OKAY.
I'M TIRED OF SEEING THIS.
I'M TIRED OF *CAUSING* IT.
IT'S A WAR. YOU DIDN'T START IT.
DIDN'T I?
NOT GOING THERE AGAIN. WILLOW GOT HER POWER BACK.
THE SAME AS SHE WAS BEFORE?
ALL OF A SUDDEN.
BUT NOT... *MORE* POWER?
SHE WASN'T DARK, IF THAT'S WHAT YOU MEAN. LOOK, SHE'S HANDLING OUR ROGUE GODDESSES. YOU SHOULD PROBABLY REST.
YOU DID WHAT YOU HAD TO, BUFF.
I'M PROUD OF YOU.

THAT'S WHAT RILEY SAID.
WELL, HE'S A BRAINY GUY.
PLUS HE'S DANGLING *STEEL,* WORKING INSIDE TWILIGHT'S CAMP.

SINCE WHEN ARE YOU SUCH A FANBOY?
YOUR ONE BOYFRIEND WH WASN'T A PSYCHO DEMON? I WAS *ALWAYS* TEAM RILEY.

THAT'S RIGHT, YOU GOT ALL TOUGH LOVE WITH ME ABOUT HIM.
LITTLE TOO LATE.
THAT'S MY MOTTO...

I'M TOO LATE AGAIN, AREN'T I?
FOR WHAT?

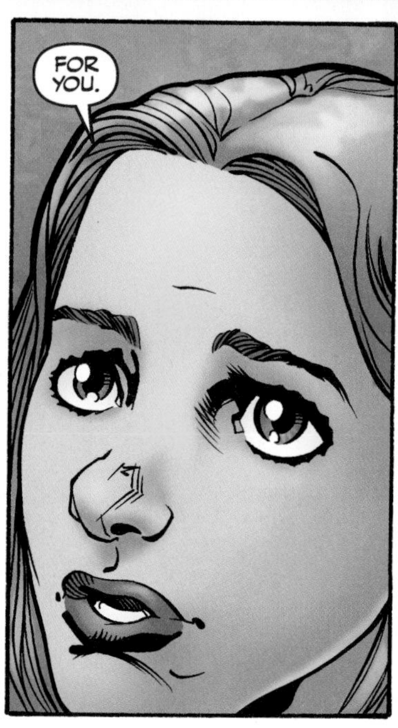
FOR YOU.

WHO TO T
HOW TO T
HAMMINA

YOU AND DAWN.
OH, IS THAT A CONVERSATION THAT'S HAPPENING?

NO, IT'S FINE. WN'S A GROWN MAN, AND YOU'RE DISGUSTING PAEDOPHILE.
CRADLE ROBBER?
WHOA!

COME ON! I AT *LEAST* GET CRADLE ROBBER...
IT IS MY BEESWAX! SHE'S MY SISTER. AND YOU AND I...
YOU GET TO MIND YOUR OWN BEESWAX.

YOU AND I WHAT? WAIT--WHAT'S *"TOO LATE AGAIN"* MEAN?
NOTHING! IT JUST... IT MEANS...
IT'S JUST...

WHAT ABOUT *ME?*

YOOOOU... HAVE FEELINGS.
AT ME.

WOULD THAT BE GOOD?

THAT WOULD BE GREAT.

IF IT WAS A BUNCH OF YEARS AGO AND YOU ACTUALLY MEANT IT.

YOU DON'T KNOW HOW--
PUH.
*LEAZE.*

FEELINGS EVELOP. PEOPLE CHANGE!
AND NOW YOU LIKE ME. I MADE THE LIST.

THERE'S NOT A--
HEY, THAT'S A BIG DEAL! I'M A POTENTIAL ROMANTIC INTEREST! I'M ON THE LIST-- RIGHT AFTER *BEING GAY.*

I RATE ALMOST AS GOOD AS TRYING TO CHANGE YOUR SEXUAL ORIENTATION. YOU WENT--
*--THROUGH GAY--*
--TO ME.

I WAS HAVING A PHASE! I'M *SUPPOSED* TO HAVE THAT PHASE!
AND NOW ALL THIS COMES TO YOU RIGHT WHEN I'M KISSING YOUR SISTER. COINCIDENCE?
*NO!* I MEAN *YES!* I MEAN IT'S BEEN... HAPPENING!
IT HAS NOTHING TO DO WITH SEEING YOU KISS.
OH YES IT DOES!

IT DOES BECAUSE EVEN IF YOU FELT SOMETHING BEFORE, ONCE YOU SAW US TOGETHER YOU SHOULD KNOW THE DECENT THING TO DO WOULD BE TO KEEP IT TO YOURSELF!
THAT IS THE MOST--

OH.

YEAH.

DAWN HAS LOVED ME HER WHOLE LIFE.
IT'S NOT UNWEIRD, KNOWING HER SINCE SHE WAS LITTLE, AND I DO FEEL A TAD BIT HUMBERT HUMBERT...
...OR HENRY HIGGINS-- I CAN NEVER REMEMBER WHICH IS WHICH...
...BUT SHE'S GROWN. AND SHRUNK. SHE'S NOT THE SAME.

I'M KIND OF IN LOVE WITH HER.
SORRY.

NO, IT'S GOOD.
I LOVE YOU BOTH. AND I'M SORRY I'M THE WORST PERSON IN THE UNIVERSE.

AH, IT'S PART OF YOUR CHARM.
YOU WON'T TELL DAWN HOW I'M THE WORST PERSON IN THE UNIVERSE?
PROMISE

AND DO I STILL GET TO MAKE CRADLE-ROBBER JOKES?
JUST USED UP YOUR LAST.

UH, *COUGH.*
NOISE OF COUGH.

HEY, DAWNIE, WE--
NOTHING! FRIEND HUG! BECAUSE OF SAD.
NO SUBTLE BOSOM-PRESSING IN HUG.

BUFFY, I'M YOUR SISTER. I KNOW YOU COULD NEVER DO ANYTHING SUBTLE.
CAT'S OUT, DAWNIE.
AND I APPROVE. I'M BUFFY AND I APPROVE THIS KISSAGE.

DIDN'T ASK, BUT OKAY. WE GOT BIGGER PROBLEMS. THREE OF THEM. GODDESS-SIZED.

WILL CAN'T CONTAIN THEM?
NOT ALONE.
I THINK I MIGHT HAVE AN IDEA.
JUST DIVING RIGHT IN TO THE P.D.A., THERE...

MY MAGIC BOUNCES OFF THEM. I'M BARELY SLOWING THEM DOWN.
COOL GIANT ASTRAL HEAD.
ARE MY NOSTRILS, LIKE, HUGE?
YOU LOOK GREAT. HERE'S THE DEAL.

DON'T FOCUS ON THEM.
THEY WERE DEEP IN THE EARTH, RIGHT? YOU JUST DIG ME A BIG HOLE.

AND WHAT, COVER IT WITH LEAVES? THESE ARE GODDESSES, NOT TIGERS.
WILL, YOU DIG, I'LL DO THE REST.

PLEASE TELL ME THIS DOESN'T INVOLVE ARTILLERY.
IT DOES NOT.
IT INVOLVES SOMETHING DON'T REALLY UNDERSTA THAT, HONESTLY, FREAKS OUT, AND I WAS HOPING NOT TO MENTION.

IT'S A NUKE.
YOU'RE A DYKE.
YOU SACRIFICE A "KEY"...
THANKS FOR THE VOTE OF NO CONFIDENCE AND SHUT YOUR MOUTHS AND LOOK.

UP IN THE SKY.

THAT'S ACTUALLY HOT.
I...DON'T AGREE.
GAPE.

SWOOSH

IF THEY STAY DORMANT, THE SLAYERS SHOULD GET THEIR POWER BACK PRETTY QUICKLY.
AND ME?
YOU I DON'T GET.
E MIGHT NEED DO TESTS. SEE XACTLY WHAT YOU ARE.
IT MIGHT RELATED TO E EVENT THAT POWERED ME, UT MY GUT SAYS NO.
XANDER AND DAWN ARE IN LOVE.
GAH! I THOUGHT THEY'D NEVER FIGURE THAT OUT.

# TWILIGHT

## CHAPTER ONE: BUFFY HAS F#©$ING SUPERPOWERS

I CAN'T HEAR YOU, DAWNIE.
MY FINGERS ARE IN MY EARS.
THEY'RE NOT IN YOUR EARS.
WHO SAID THAT?
XANDER. BUFFY'S BEST FRIEND. ONE EYE. FUNNY. MOSTLY.
BUFF, IT'S TIME...
DAWN. BUFFY'S SISTER. WAS A GIANT, A CENTAUR, A LITTLE DOLL. NOT ANYMORE. (OBVIOUSLY.)

LET ME JUST SAY... AND NO PRESSURE HERE--
--BUT IF THIS WORKS, THIS COULD QUITE POSSIBLY BE--
PRESSURE. BEING FELT.
PRESSURE INCREASING.
--THIS W
BE MORE V
TO ME THAN
OWN BIRT
BUF
SLA
STA

WHOSE GUN IS THAT?
YOU KEEP FORGETTING I CARRY A GUN.
I DON'T LIKE THEM. THEY KEEP KILLING MY FRIENDS.
YOU READY FOR THIS OR NOT?

MY NAME IS BUFFY SUMMERS.
ON YOUR MARK...!
BUFFY, YOU NEED TO SQUAT DOWN.
SHOULD I SQUAT, OR DO IT FROM STANDING?
I THINK IT LOOKS COOLER FR
STANDING
NO. SQUAT, FOR SURE.
SQUAT EQUALS RACING.

FOR MONTHS NOW, I'VE BEEN FIGHTING SOME LOONY BIRD NAMED TWILIGHT.
GET SET...!
YOU'RE RIGHT, SQUAT IS BETTER.

GO!
YESTERDAY I SOMEHOW GOT SUPER POWERS.
MY FRIENDS KEEP ASKING ME HOW IT FEELS.
WHAT'RE YOU DOING?!
GIVING IT A HEAD START.

ARE YOU--? RUN!
WE'RE NOT EVEN SURE YOU'RE THAT FA--

S

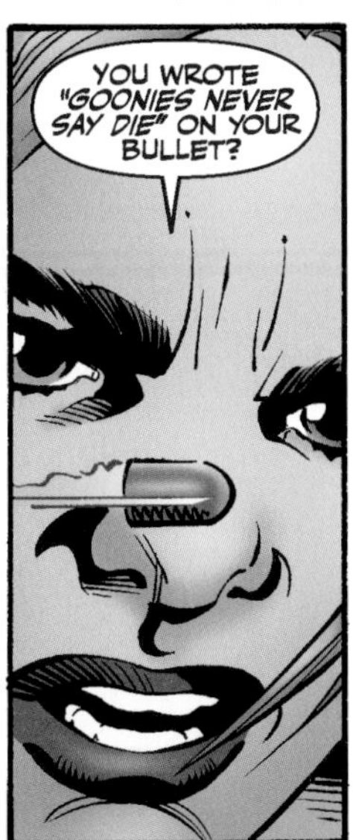
YOU WROTE "GOONIES NEVER SAY DIE" ON YOUR BULLET?

HOW DO THEY THINK IT FEELS?

T.
IT FEELS...

BUGS. IN TEETH.
NOT FUN.
YOU BEAT IT.
NEAT, HUH?
NO...

"...HERE'S NEAT."
WHAT LOOKS BETTER? ONE HAND OR TWO?
WHERE'D YOU GET A TRAIN?
FROM THE CASTLE.
IN THE GARDEN.
PUT IT BACK!
DON'T WORRY...

"...THAT'S EXACTLY WHERE WE'RE HEADED."
DEFINITELY TALL.
REALLY TALL.
AND CONVENIENTLY LOCATED RIGHT WHERE WE ARE IN TIBET.
THINK YOU CAN MAKE IT?
I'LL MAKE IT.
GOOD. BECAUSE...
HHUUUUF!
WHAT'RE YOU DOING?
YOU'VE GOT ME?
WHO'S GOT...
YOOOOOOOOOOOOOOOOOU?!
THOOM
HAT TRICK.
"I'M TELLING YOU, WILLOW, THIS IS BAD..."
WHOOMP

DOESN'T SOUND BAD.
WILLOW. BUFFY'S BEST FRIEND. ALSO A WITCH. IN FUTURE, GOES DARK PHOENIX. WE THINK.
NO. TRUST ME. BAD.
REMEMBER WHEN I GOT POWERS--?
YOU DIDN'T GET POWERS.
YOU BECAME A GIANT. THEN A HORSE--
A CENTAURETTE.
CENTAURETTE?
GIRL CENTAUR. THERE'S A DIFFERENCE.

DAWNIE, WATCH OUT--CANDLE FLOATING BEHIND YOU...
HAVE YOU SEEN THEM OUT THERE? THEY'RE TREATING IT LIKE IT'S A JOKE.

EVEN ANDREW WOULD TAKE IT MORE SERIOUS THAN THAT.
ANDREW'S NOT WITH THEM?
HUH. ODD.
NO, WHAT'S ODD IS WHEN YOU IGNORE THE FACT THAT YOU DON'T GET POWER FOR FREE.
MINE WAS A CURSE FROM A THRICEWISE!

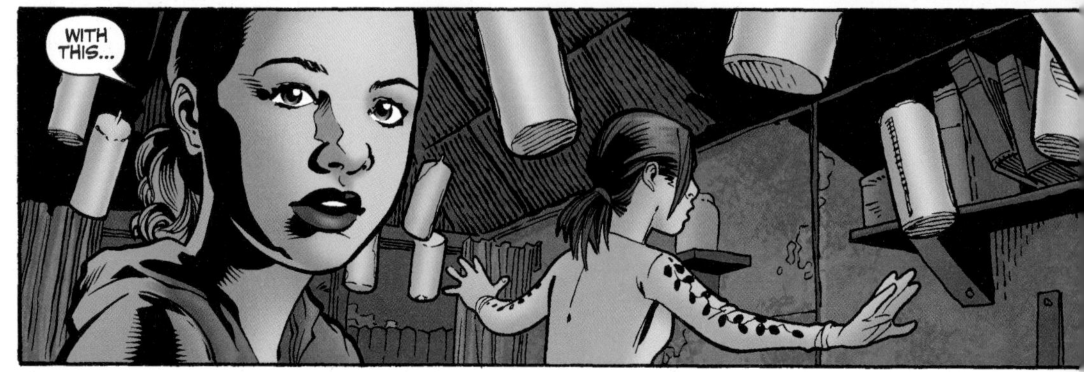
WITH THIS...

.WHO KNOWS HAT THEY'VE NLEASHED?"
OKAY OKAY OKAY.
OKAY.
OKAY.
BREATHE.
OKAY.
TRY HEAT VISION.

NOTHING.
X-RAY VISION?
NOTHING.
OOH, OOH-- TRY PENETRA-VISION!
WHAT'S PENETRA-VISION?
IT'S X-RAY VISION! JUST TRY IT!

SATSU, Y SIGN OF ANDREW?
LAST I HEARD, E WAS PAINTING MAGIC LASSO FOR BUFFY.
HOW ABOUT GILES OR FAITH?
WILL CHECK.
AM I THE ONLY ONE WHO SEES THE REAL PROBLEM HERE?
DAWNIE, MAYBE YOU JUST MISS YOUR OWN POWERS.

YOU JUST SAID--
I DIDN'T HAVE POWERS! XANDER DOESN'T HAVE POWERS.
YES, BUT RIGHT NOW, XANDER HAS BUFFY.
IN FACT...

.YOU SURE HAT'S NOT HE REAL ROBLEM?"
TRY READING MY MIND.
I CAN! IT SAYS...
SO MUCH... MASTURBATION.
SWEET MOTHER OF SHIRLEY HEMPHILL, IS THAT THE BEST YOU CAN DO? REALLY?

NO, NO... BUFFY AND XANDER...
THEY HAD THIS BIG TALK...MADE PEACE--
--IT WAS ALL VERY NICE.
GOOD. THEN YOU NEED TO UNDERSTAND-- ALTHOUGH WE WERE FIST-FIGHTING THOSE GODDESSES FOR NEARLY FORTY-EIGHT HOURS STRAIGHT--
--IT DOESN'T MEAN THAT EVERY MONTH-- ON EVERY WEDNESDAY-- IT HAS TO BE THE END OF THE WORLD.
THAT'S NOT TRUE. HAVEN'T YOU EVER READ "THE MONKEY'S PAW"?

"YOU DON'T GET THE GOOD WITHOUT GETTING THE CURSE."
TELEPORTATION?
NO.
SUPER-BREATH?
NO.
ADAMANTIUM CLAWS?
XANDER...
CAN YOU SHOOT ARROWS?
THAT'S NOT EVEN A POWER.
SOLVE A MYSTERY?
NOT A POWER.
SPIN A WEB ANY SIZE?
WHY WOULD I EVEN WANNA DO THAT?
TO CATCH THIEVES, JUST LIKE FLIES.
WAIT, CAN YOU BUILD A SUIT OF ARMOR?
THIS IS STARTING TO NOT BE FUN ANYMORE.
I GOT IT!

CAN YOU PHASE?

ORRY, WILL-- IEY WERE ALL ERE EARLIER, BUT RIGHT NOW--
--NO SIGN OF GILES OR FAITH EITHER.
DAWNIE, I HEAR YOU. I DO. BUT BUFFY'S ALWAYS HAD POWERS.
NOT LIKE THESE. NOW SHE'S FASTER THAN A SPEEDING--
OH, JEEZ, I JUST REALIZED WHAT THEY WERE DOING. LOSERS.
BUFFY DEFEATED THREE POWERFUL GODDESSES...

I'M SURE THIS IS JUST THE NIVERSE'S EMPORARY REWARD."
WHATTYA MEAN, "PHASE"?
YOU SORTA... YOU PUT YOUR ARM OUT AND YOU KINDA... IT GOES RIGHT THROUGH THE WALL.
LIKE A GHOST?
BUT THEN WOULDN'T YOU FALL THROUGH THE FLOOR?

NO--BECAUSE YOU CAN CONTROL YOUR MOLECULES...AND MESS UP MACHINERY AND-- AND--AND--
--AND YOU'RE REALLY CUTE, AND YOU HAVE THIS SPUNKY PERSONALITY AND YOU'RE NOT AFRAID OF THE TOUGH GUYS WHO EVERYONE ELSE IS TERRIFIED OF.
IT'S GOOD STUFF.

I DON'T SEE THE APPEAL.

WILL, PLEASE-- JUST STOP. LOOK AT WHAT'S HAPPENING. YOU OF ALL PEOPLE.
THE MORE POWER BUFFY GETS--
WHY'RE YOU FLOATING THERE ANYWAY?
JUST A CALLING SPELL-- WE KNOW THEY'RE NOT AMONG THE DEAD.
VANSHANTU NAHCANTU PREESBI...
YOU OF ALL PEOPLE, WILL--YOU KNOW WHAT'S GONNA HAPPEN TO HER. THE MORE POWER SHE GETS--
"--THE BIGGER THE MONSTERS WE'LL HAVE TO FIGHT."
7.2 MILES AWAY.
NORTHERN CLIFFSIDES.
THEY STILL CAN'T SEE US?
NOT FROM THIS DISTANCE.

YOU DON'T KNOW THAT. THESE NEW POWERS SHE'S DISPLAYING...
AMY. BAD GIRL. BAD WITCH. WAS A RAT. CRAVES CHEESE.
SHE'S GOT POWERS?
WARREN, ARE YOU BLIND? SHE'S FASTER THAN A SPEEDING--
OH. I JUST REALIZED WHAT THEY WERE DOING. NERD-A-TRONS.
WARREN. BAD GUY. NO SKIN. EASILY SLIGHTED. NERDY.
THINK SHE CAN PHASE?
THE GENERAL. NAME CLASSIFIED. LIKE OTHERS, WORKS FOR TWILIGHT. ALSO CRAVES CHEESE.
WHAT ABOUT THE WITCH?
SHE'S NOT LOOKING FOR US...
"SHE DOESN'T EVEN KNOW IT'S HAPPENED YET."
YOU'RE NOT EVEN LISTENING ANYMORE, ARE YOU, WILL?
SKUANTUU VLADATETH...
...EKANUU
OY.

NOW LOOK P AT THE SKY ND SHOUT IT LIKE THIS:
"SPOON!"
BUFFY, WE GOT PROBLEMS!

I SEARCHED FOR THEM--THEY'RE NOT HERE.
WHO'S NOT HERE?

SEE, THE MONKEY'S PAW IS STARTING! JUST LIKE I SAID!
DAWN!
WHO'S NOT HERE, WILL?

SEE, XAN? IT NEVER STOPS.
NO ONE'S LISTENING TO A WORD I'M--
YOU THINK IT'D BE HARD TO MAKE A SIGNAL WATCH?

GILES, ANDREW, FAITH.
AFTER THE BATTLE--
--THEY WERE HERE. NOW THEY'RE GONE.
DID YOU--?
ALREADY DID A SPELL.
I THINK THEY WERE TELEPORTED.
I THOUGHT YOU MAGICKED US IN? NO TELEPORTING IN OR OUT.
THEY WERE TAKEN OUTSIDE THE PERIMETER FIRST.

CHECK BEYOND THE CAMP.
DID THAT TOO. MAYBE SOMETHING'S HIDING THEM.
THEN DO THE UNHIDING-THEM SPELL.
THE WAY WE'RE HATED THESE DAYS...

"...IT'S NOT SAFE OUT THERE."

THE WITCH KNOWS. AND SHE KNOWS HOW WE GOT IN.
UNCLEAR...
THAT GOOD OR BAD? WE'RE ALMOST THERE.

"...BUT I THINK WE'RE ABOUT TO FIND OUT."

I ASSUME YOU'RE LOOKING FOR GILES FIRST?
FAITH.
EVEN WITH THE EXTRA SLAYERS, SHE'S STILL EASIEST TO FIND.
SHUUNATI FUUG GHALLGAH DER SHTUUL.

AIT. I KNOW WHAT THAT EANS. I CAN NDERSTAND IT.
"TAKE ME TO THE SLAYER WHO NEEDS ME MOST."
MAYBE IT'S YOUR NEW POWERS.

THAT'S FINE--BUT, WILL--
I THOUGHT *I* WAS THE SLAYER WHO NEEDS YOU MOST?
BE SERIOUS, BUFFY...

YOU HAVE FRIENDS.
PIP

NO MORE WILLOW.
WE'RE CLOSE. LESS THAN THREE KLICKS AWAY.
ARE KLICKS FAR? IS THAT A LOT?
FIRE IT UP, PEOPLE. WITH THE WITCH OUT...
"...THIS MIGHT ACTUALLY WORK."
KUALA LUMPUR, MALAYSIA.
UNNUMBERED APARTMENT BUILDING.
THIRD FLOOR.
PIP
I DON'T LIKE TELEPORTING.
MAKES ME GASSY.
I ALSO DON'T LIKE 'PORTING INTO STRANGE PLACES THAT SMELL LIKE OLD EGGS, URINE, AND RUSTY PENNIES.
FAITH...?
FAITH, YOU OKAY?
BUT WHAT I LIKE LEAST IS... THAT SMELL...
IT AIN'T EGGS.
MY GODDESS.

WHERE'S BUFF--?

--Y?
YOU DID THAT ON PURPOSE.

I CHECKED ALL OF GILES'S SAFEHOUSES.
BUDAPEST?
BUDAPEST, ENGLAND, THE U.K.--
ENGLAND'S IN THE U.K.

OKAY, XAN, WE GET YOU'RE ALL MILITARY NOW. I EVEN CHECKED THE ONE IN BRUSSELS. Y'KNOW THEY HAVE BUNNIES INSTEAD OF SQUIRRELS?
HOW'D YOU GET THERE SO FAST?
SHE RAN.
I FLEW.
WHAT? WOULD YOU RUN IF YOU COULD FLY?

STILL NO TELESCOPIC VISION?
I TRIED. NO EYE POWERS.
BUT IF WE'RE LUCKY...

"...HOPEFULLY WILLOW'LL TURN UP SOMETHING."
FLORIDA.
THE PORT OF MIAMI.
CONTAINER # 601174-7.
PIP
THIS ONE'S WORSE.
THE SMELL IS ALL METAL.

METAL OUTSIDE.
METAL INSIDE.
Vamps
Die Slayers!
THGIL.
THE LIGHT SHOWS ME WHAT I'M LOOKING FOR.

FROM THE DENTS IN THE WALL, I KNOW IT WAS A HELL OF A FIGHT.
FROM THE SKIN COLOR, I KNOW IT'S NOT A VAMP.
ANDREW, IF YOU'RE ALIVE AND THIS IS SOME JOKE FOR YOUTUBE...
...I PROMISE YOU, THAT COFFIN'LL BE YOURS.

AND FROM WHAT'S INSIDE, I KNOW GILES AND FAITH AND ANDREW...

E SCREWED.
GILES. BUFFY'S WATCHER. TOUCHES GLASSES A LOT. GROWN UP.
FAITH. BECAME SLAYER WHEN BUFFY DIED. NOT SO THRILLED SHE CAME BACK. SLUTTY FOR ATTENTION.
ANDREW. THAT'S ME!
--CUZ YOU KNOW I'M IN LOVE WITH AN UPTOWN GIRL... MY UP-TOWN GUUUURL!
W-WHAT'S HAPPENED? WHERE ARE WE?
UHHHH...
...I'M... MAN, I'M GASSY.
SOMEONE NEEDS TO GET PUNCHED FOR THAT.
BE THAT AS IT MAY...
...ANY IDEA WHAT'S--?
SUFFERIN' SAPPHO.
HE DID IT...
THE DUAL COMPARTMENTS... THE SIMONSON DESIGN...
I BET HE DID FROZEN VALENCES!

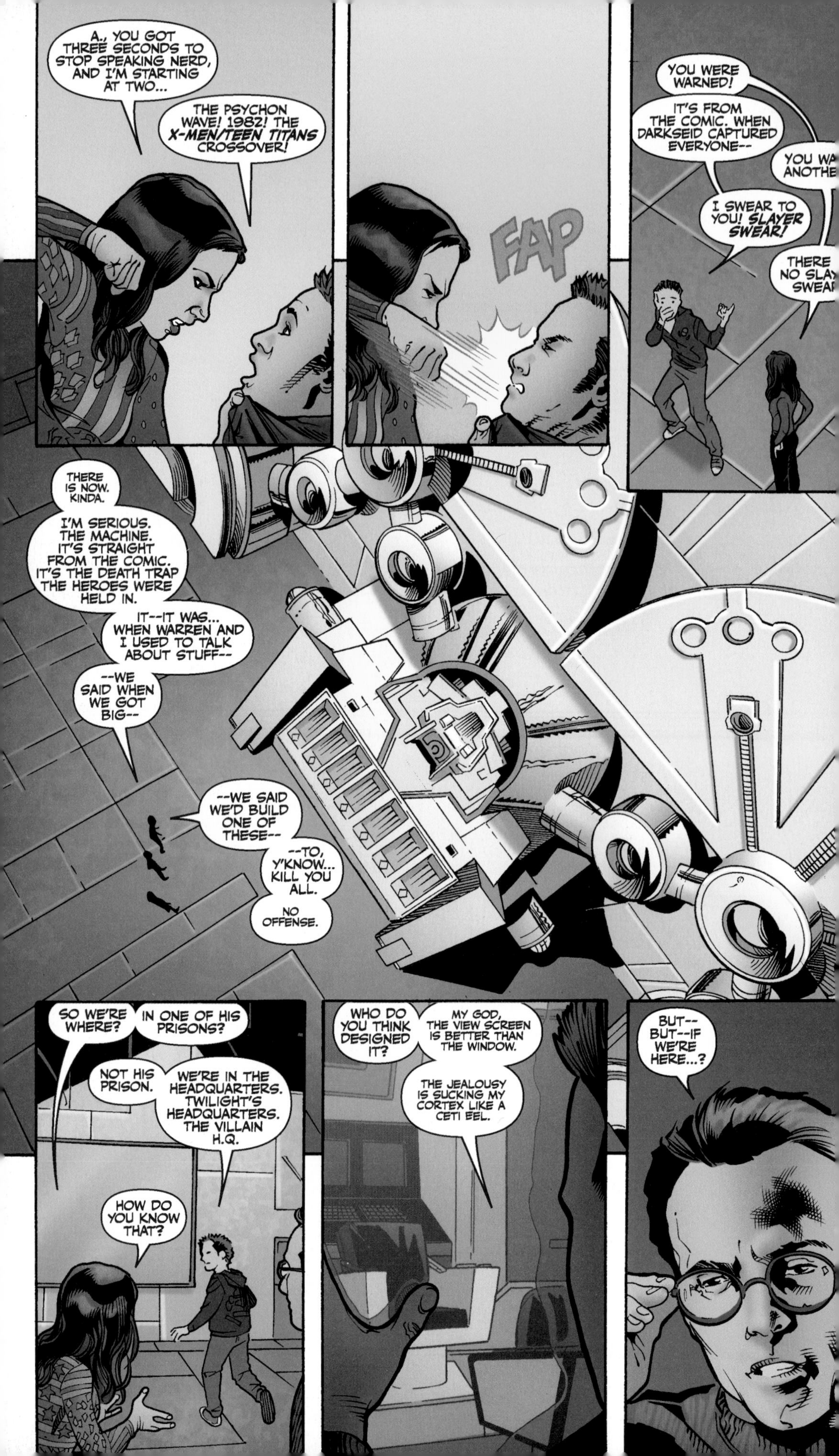
A., YOU GOT THREE SECONDS TO STOP SPEAKING NERD, AND I'M STARTING AT TWO...
THE PSYCHON WAVE! 1982! THE *X-MEN/TEEN TITANS* CROSSOVER!
FAP
YOU WERE WARNED!
IT'S FROM THE COMIC. WHEN DARKSEID CAPTURED EVERYONE--
I SWEAR TO YOU! *SLAYER SWEAR!*
THERE IS NOW. KINDA.
I'M SERIOUS. THE MACHINE. IT'S STRAIGHT FROM THE COMIC. IT'S THE DEATH TRAP THE HEROES WERE HELD IN.
IT--IT WAS... WHEN WARREN AND I USED TO TALK ABOUT STUFF--
--WE SAID WHEN WE GOT BIG--
--WE SAID WE'D BUILD ONE OF THESE--
--TO, Y'KNOW... KILL YOU ALL.
NO OFFENSE.
SO WE'RE WHERE?
IN ONE OF HIS PRISONS?
NOT HIS PRISON.
WE'RE IN THE HEADQUARTERS. TWILIGHT'S HEADQUARTERS. THE VILLAIN H.Q.
HOW DO YOU KNOW THAT?
WHO DO YOU THINK DESIGNED IT?
MY GOD, THE VIEW SCREEN IS BETTER THAN THE WINDOW.
THE JEALOUSY IS SUCKING MY CORTEX LIKE A CETI EEL.
BUT--BUT--IF WE'RE HERE...?

"...WHERE IN
EAVEN'S NAME
IS EVERYONE
ELSE?"
MORGAN CITY, LOUISIANA.
THE ATCHAFALAYA BASIN.
UNNAMED MARSH.
PIP
IT'S THE SAME AS BEFORE.
FOUL SMELL.
ODD PLACE.
AND DEAD--
NO. NOT DEAD YET.
H-H-HELP... HELP ME...
I-I KNOW YOU-- YOU'RE A SLAYER.
HOW DO I KNOW YOU...?
...AT TRAINING... IN ATLANTA...
KOFF
...CORI... MY NAME'S CORI...
I CAN DO A HEALING SPELL, CORI.
...YOU CAN'T... YOU KNOW YOU CAN'T...
...THEY FOUND US... BUT THE MOB...
...THEY WERE A MOB...
I DON'T UNDERSTAND...
WHO'S "US"?
WHO WERE YOU WITH?
ALL OF US...
...ALL OUR GIRLS.
...JUST PLEASE...

"...PLEASE DON'T TELL BUFFY WE FAILED..."
I HAVE TELESCOPIC VISION!
SAYS WHAT?
I CAN SEE...
IT'S HARD TO TURN IT OFF.
IN GREECE... MYKONOS
THERE'S AN OLDER COUPL WHO--

EW.
EW, LIKE INTERNET EW!
THAT'LL LEARN YA.
YOU CAN'T UNSEE WHAT YOU SEE.

TRY FOCUSING IT AROUND HERE.
MAYBE GILES AND FAITH ARE STILL ON THIS SIDE OF THE CLIFFS.
WHAT? YOU FOUND THEM?
I'LL CHECK, BUT--
OOOH.
NOT THEM...

"...BUT I DEFINITELY FOUND SOMEONE."
I THINK SHE'S COMING.
EXCUSE ME?
SHE. HER.
BUFFY.
RUN.

"RUN"? SHE'S TWO MILES AWAY.
I CAN DO A SPELL.
NOT THAT FAST YOU CAN'T.
THERE'S NO RETREAT.
YOU UNDERSTAND? WE FIGHT UNTIL--!
SHE CAN SEE US. CAN SHE SEE US?
GENERAL... WOULD YOU CARE TO STEP OUTSIDE?

FREEZE!
I SAID FREEZE!
THEY HEARD YOU, XAN.
THEY DID?
SEE? FREEZING.

OKAY. THAT'S GOOD.
BUT...
ER...
AREN'T YOU A SUPERVILLAIN TEAM TRYING TO MURDER US?

WHAT? NOW YOU DON'T WANT TO MURDER US?
WE'RE NOT A SUPERVILLAIN TEAM. WE JUST HAVE A MILITARY GUY.
AND A SQUABBLING COUPLE.
WE DON'T SQUABBLE.

WE DIDN'T COME TO ATTACK.
I THOUGHT TWILIGHT--
DON'T YOU SEE...?
TWILIGHT KICKED US OUT--
HE USED US.
I DON'T LIKE BEING USED.
HE DOESN'T. AND I DON'T LIKE IT EVEN MORE.
SO IF YOU HELP US--

--WE'LL HELP YOU KICK HIS ASS.

PIP

B--!

WILL?

--UFFY!
OH.
YOU'RE GETTING FASTER.

Y'THINK?
MONKEY'S PAW!

DAWN'S RIGHT! THIS IS ALL--IT'S NO GOOD.
I CAN FEEL IT. SOMETHING REALLY BAD'S ABOUT TO HAPPEN.
I THOUGHT YOU WERE LOOKING FOR GILES AND FAITH?
I WAS. I TRIED.
BUT INSTEAD--
BUFFY, YOUR POWERS-- THEY'RE NOT A GIFT FOR DEFEATING THE GODDESSES.
WHAT'RE YOU TALKING ABOUT?

WHEN WE WERE FIGHTING-- THOSE FORTY-EIGHT HOURS WE WERE OUT--
--SO MANY SLAYERS--
--THERE WERE ATTACKS ALL OVER, AND I FOUND...
WILL, YOU'RE SCARING ME...
YOU NEED TO BE SCARED.
DON'T YOU SEE? ALL THE GIRLS WHO DIED FIGHTING HERE, PLUS OUT THERE...
ALL TH POWER

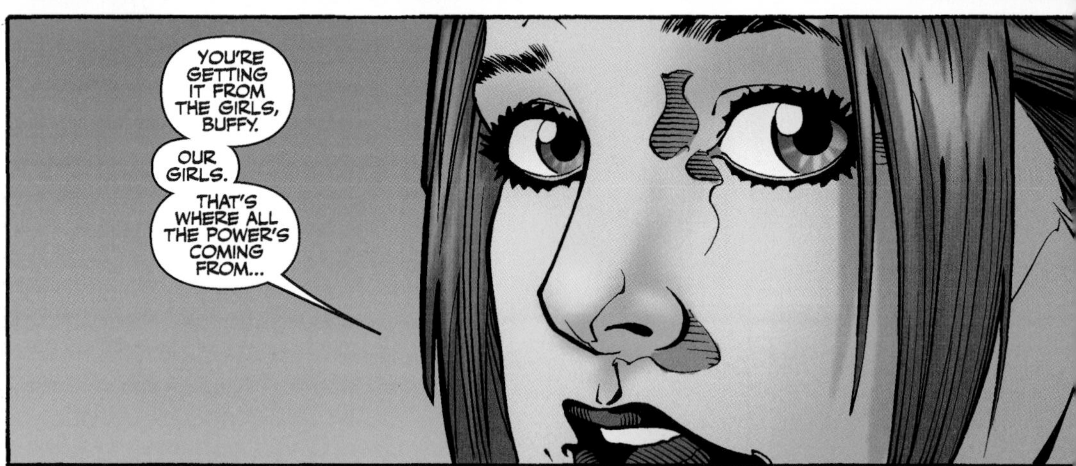
YOU'RE GETTING IT FROM THE GIRLS, BUFFY.
OUR GIRLS.
THAT'S WHERE ALL THE POWER'S COMING FROM...

YOU'RE SUCKING IT FROM EVERY SLAYER WHO DIES.
"HERE'S MY TRUE CONCERN--"

--WHEN WE SET UP CAMP, WILLOW'S MAGICKS WERE PROTECTING US, YES?
SO FOR TWILIGHT TO TELEPORT US HERE--
AMY DID IT.
SHE TELEPORTED THRE OF US OUT, WHICH LE HER PORT THREE O THEM IN. THAT'S WH NO ONE'S HERE.
WARREN WAS WORKIN ON A SIMIL TRANSPORTE FOR YEARS

STUPID WARREN-- EVEN USED THE SAME PASS CODES.
J-Ø-S-H-U-A. PLEASE.
OKAY, SO THREE OF US COME HERE, BUT I THOUGHT RILEY SAID THERE WERE FOUR.
FOUR WHAT?
FOUR. OF THEM.
FOUR BAD GUYS, RIGHT?
AMY, WARREN, THE GENERAL, AND--
SWSHHHH
HE CAN SEE US. CAN HE SEE US?
YOU CAN CALL ME TWILIGHT.
NOW WHO WANTS TO HEAR A REALLY COOL MASTER PLAN?
Next: The Master Plan

# TWILIGHT

## CHAPTER TWO: THE MASTER PLAN

IT REALLY IS THE BEST SNACK EVER.
NOT FUNNY, XAN.

WASN'T TRYING TO BE FUNNY.
OH, THE EYE PATCH. PIRATE.
THAT'S *KINDA* FUNNY.
(AND OVERUSED.)

IT'S *NOT* FUNNY.
AND Y'KNOW I HATE PEP TALKS.
YOU *LOVE* PEP TALKS.
OUR BEST MOMENTS HAVE BEEN PEP TALKS.
BUT THIS ISN'T THAT MOMENT.
DIDN'T YOU HEAR WHAT WILLOW SAID? THE ONLY REASON I CAN DO--

--THIS--
--IS BECAUSE I'M TAKING THE POWER FROM OTHER SLAYERS.
NO. NONONO. YOU'RE NOT TAKING THEIR POWERS-- YOU'RE--
--YOU'RE GETTING THEIR POWER WHEN THEY DIE. LIKE HIGHLANDER. OR RISING STARS.
BOY, THAT'S NOT A GOOD PEP TALK.

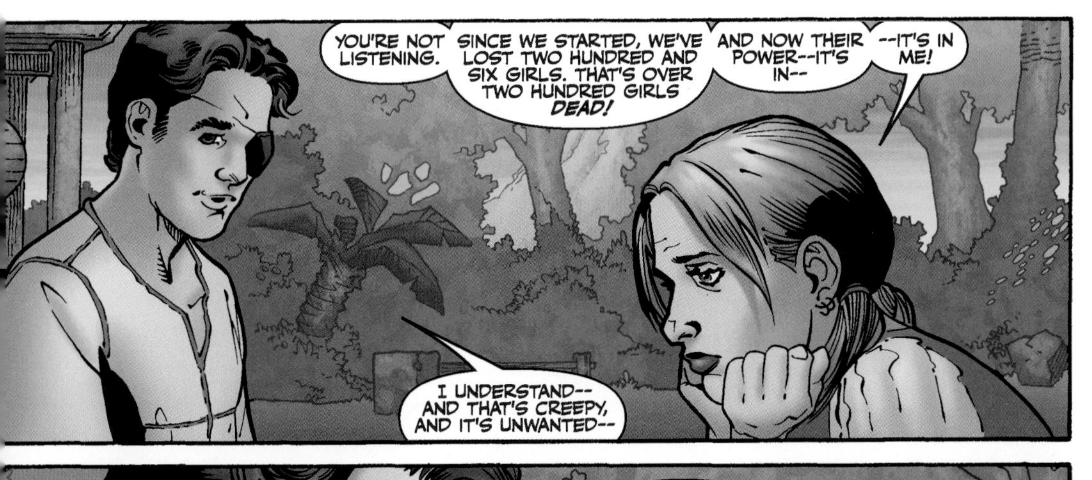
YOU'RE NOT LISTENING.
SINCE WE STARTED, WE'VE LOST TWO HUNDRED AND SIX GIRLS. THAT'S OVER TWO HUNDRED GIRLS *DEAD!*
AND NOW THEIR POWER--IT'S IN--
--IT'S IN ME!
I UNDERSTAND-- AND THAT'S CREEPY, AND IT'S UNWANTED--

--BUT IT DOESN'T MAKE YOU A BAD PERSON.

BUT DON'T YOU SEE WHAT IT DOES MAKE ME?
IF I'M SUCKING THEIR POWER...
IT MAKES ME A VAMPIRE.

VILLAIN H.Q.
OKAY, I'M THINKING OF A NUMBER.
WHO WANTS TO DIE FIRST?
SHOULD IT BE GILES?
FAITH?
OR...
OR...
THAT'S THE SECO TIME.
ANDREW
MY NAME ANDREW.
TH-THAT VOICE.
I KNOW THAT VOICE...
OF COURSE YOU DO, GILES...
THAT'S WHAT HAPPE WHEN YOU RID OF YO RESIDEN WITCH...

PLE START
SEEING
E TRUTH."
YOU'RE NOT A VAMPIRE.
I'M SUCKING THEIR POWERS.
THEN I GET STRONGER.
WHAT'S THAT SOUND LIKE TO YOU?

IT SOUNDS LIKE THE ONE PERSON IN THE WORLD WHO, AS ALWAYS, IS CAPABLE OF ANYTHING--
--TRULY ANYTHING THIS TIME--
--EXCEPT FORGIVING HERSELF.

AND YES, I'VE SEEN WHAT YOU CAN DO.
FLYING... SUPERSPEED...
I SAW YOU KICK THAT GIANT BOULDER LIKE A SOCCER BALL.
BUT IF THE UNIVERSE IS GIVING YOU THAT POWER, IT'S GOTTA BE FOR A REASON.
THAT'S WHY YOU WERE CHOSEN IN THE FIRST PLACE. DON'T YOU SEE?
YOU. ARE. HERE. FOR. A. REASON--
--AND IT'S NOT JUST TO KICK GIANT BOULDERS.

THAT WAS A MUCH BETTER PEP TALK.
IT WAS ACTUALLY FROM SUPERMAN I. PA KENT'S SPEECH.
GETS ME EVERY TIME.
SORRY-- IT'S JUST SO EASY WITH THE SUPERPOWER THING.

, WE'RE
OSING
TIME.
YOUR SUPERMAN SPEECH WORK OR NOT?
WILL, DON'T GO GIANT HEAD. GIANT HEADS ARE BAD.
JUST TELL ME WHAT WE'RE DOING.
SAME THING WE ALWAYS DO, PINKY. FIND THE BIG BAD...

"...AND KICK HIM IN THE BOULDERS."
YOU'RE DEAD!

YOU'RE RIGHT.

DO YOU NOT UNDERSTAND THIS ISN'T A FAIR FIGHT?

WHO SAID I WAS FIGHTING FAIR?

AND WHAT MAKES YOU THINK "INVULNERABLE" ISN'T "ALL OVER"?

"WE NEED A BETTER PLAN."

'S THE R PLAN. DING TAKES ME.
ESPECIALLY...
COUGH AMY COUGH
...SLOPPY MAGIC.
SLOPPY?
YOU'RE JUST JEALOUS YOU DIDN'T THINK OF HIDING YOUR SECRET H.Q. THREE SECONDS IN THE FUTURE.
STILL A RAT.
STILL A BITCH.
SO WHEN THE CLOAK DROPS, THEIR H.Q. WILL APPEAR ON THIS SCREEN?
THEN YOU JUST FLY IN AND DO THE FIGHT-SCENE THING.
H-HE HURT FAITH.
HOW DO YOU KNOW?
I FEEL HER. I CAN FEEL THE OTHER SLAYERS OUT THERE.
OKAY. WEIRD...
JUST DON'T FORGET WHAT WARREN SAID ABOUT THE HIDDEN ARSENAL."
--MY H.Q.! IT WAS MY GENIUS THAT BUILT IT!
AND FOR TWILIGHT TO THINK HE CAN STEAL IT FROM ME--!
RELAX, SOLDIER. WE'LL BE BACK ON TRACK SOON ENOUGH.
ACK ON CK"? YOU STENING THESE TWADS?
I MEAN, WARREN...THE GENERAL...
...THEY'VE ALL TRIED TO KILL US.
I HEAR YOU, DAWNIE.
BUT BEFORE WE DEAL WITH PROBLEM NUMBER TWO--

"--WE FIRST GOTTA DEAL WITH PROBLEM NUMBER ONE."
FAITH...?
OH C'MON, YOU'RE STRONG THAN THAT.
FAITH...?
NISCAATUU SKUANTEE VEENAA...
LACE UP YOUR SKATES, PEOPLE.
REEMERGENCE UNDERWAY...
I-INVULNERABLE...
HE'S INVULNERABLE.
AND-- AND FASTER THAN...
SUPERSPEED PLUS STRENGT
I CAN FLY TOO. YOU KNOW WHERE THIS IS HEADED, RIGHT?
I'M GETTING OUTLINES!
GET READY, BUFFY!

ERY WATCHER WONDERS F HIS SLAYER MIGHT BE THE GIRL...
...AND YOU'VE AD MORE REASON THAN ANY.

THREE SECONDS...

W-WHUT'S HE TALKING ABOUT, G.?

WAIT.
YOU HAVEN'T EVEN *TOLD* HER YET, HAVE YOU?

AND YOU HAVEN'T TOLD *BUFFY* EITHER.
I FIGURED WITH ALL YOUR RECENT JAUNTS... TO ENGLAND...TO GERMANY...
...I THOUGHT THEY ALL KNEW WHAT YOU WERE REALLY LOOKING FOR.
BUT NOW, THANKS TO YOUR SILENCE--

"--SHE HAS NO IDEA WHAT SHE'S BECOME."
--TWO SECONDS...!
BUT YOU KNOW.
SHE'S ABOUT TO FACE SOMETHING SHE TRULY CAN'T FIGHT.
NO MATTER HOW MUCH SHE--
boink
ANDREW...
DID YOU JUST HIT ME WITH A FRISBEE?
IT'S CLOBBERIN' TIME.

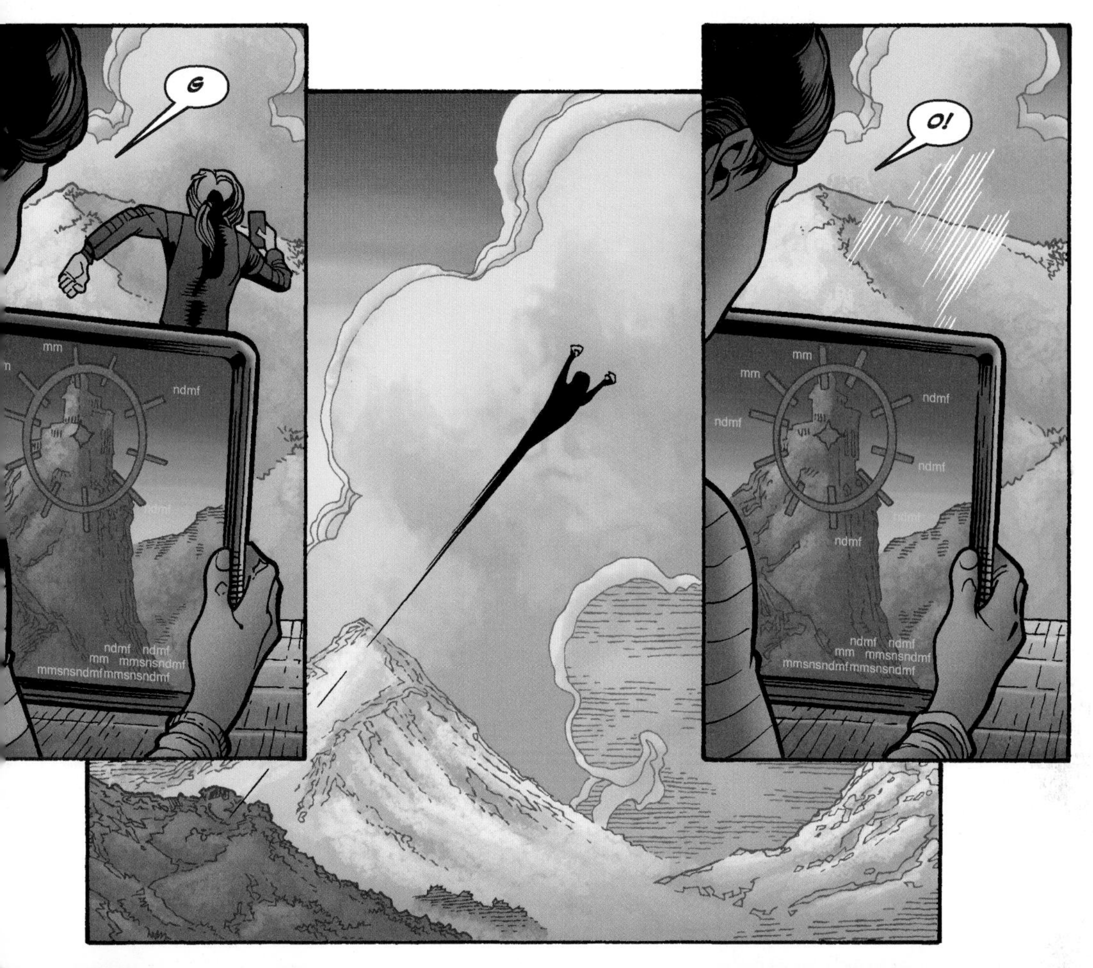
G
O!

ANDREW...
DON'T MAKE ME REPULSOR YOU, MAN!
I MIGHT MAKE YOU.

RRRRRRRR

ROOOMM!
MOMENTUM'S ON MY SIDE.
I CAUGHT HIM OFF GUARD.
YEAH...

LISTEN TO ME, TWILIGHT--
MY GOD, IS T REALLY THE E YOU PICKED? IGHT? Y'KNOW VED THAT IDEA RST, RIGHT?
AND AMPIRE GO MUCH TTER.)

I MISSED YOU TOO.

DID WE WIN?
HIS VOICE...
HE'S ANGEL... TWILIGHT IS ANGEL.
SHE'LL BEAT HIM. SHE WILL.
NO. NOT THIS TIME.
REGARDLESS OF WHAT BUFFY DOES--

"--THERE IS NO WINNING."
BUFF?
I KNOW YOU'RE OUT THERE.

YOU'RE EVEN STRONGER THAN I'D HOPED.
THAT WAS THE FIRST BLOW I'VE *FELT* IN A LONG WHILE.
BUT YOU NEED TO STOP. YOU NEED TO THINK ABOUT WHAT'S HAPPENED.

THAT'S NOT ANGEL. IT'S NOT.
IT'S GOTTA BE ANGELUS.

AND DON'T THINK I'M ANGELUS EITHER.
I'M ME.
AND YOU KNOW I'M ME. I KNOW YOU FEEL IT.

OH, AND BUFF--
STOP TALKING!
YOUR BEST ASSET WAS THAT YOU WEREN'T A TALKER!

KRRRKKK
WHAT WAS THAT?
THAT WAS A SONIC BOOM.
I THINK THEY'RE FIGHTING.
YOU KILLED MY GIRLS!
TWO HUNDRED AND SIX GIRLS!

DIDN'T KILL
ONE. THIS WAS
HAPPENING.
STOP SAYING CRYPTIC CRAP LIKE THAT!
IT HAPPENED BECAUSE YOU MADE IT HAPPEN! YOU MADE THEM HATE US!
YOU REALLY DON'T KNOW HOW MUCH WORSE IT COULD'VE BEEN?
POWERFUL PEOPLE-- GOVERNMENTS-- LINING UP TO WIPE OUT THE "TERRORISTS" YOU CREATED. DEMONS WEREN'T THRILLED EITHER.
UFF!
I PUT ON A MASK, TALK ABOUT "MASTER PLANS"... DISTRACT THEM. KEEP THE BODY COUNT AS LOW AS I CAN WHILE I PUSH.

PUSH ME WHY? SO I CAN ABSORB THE POWER OF MY DEAD FRIENDS?
WHO TOLD YOU THAT? WILLOW? I THOUGHT SHE'D SEE FURTHER THAN THAT.
THAT'S NOT WHY YOU HAVE THESE POWERS.
AND STOP TRYING TO PUNCH ME.
HUUF!
IT WON'T MAKE YOU FEEL BETTER.

IT WILL.

BAM

SEE? IT WON'T. NOT THIS TIME.
NOT IF YOU HIT ME A HUNDRED TIMES.
IT'S DIFFERENT NOW, BUFFY.
YOUR POWER-- LIKE MY POWER--HAS NOTHING TO DO WITH THE OTHER SLAYERS.
WHAT'S HAPPENING TO YOU--TO US--
--THIS IS WHAT WE'VE BEEN WAITING FOR.
WHAT WE EARNED. WHAT WE NEED.

STOP LYING TO ME! I KNOW YOU'RE LYING!
WHY ELSE WOULD YOU BE-BE-BE--
--BE HIDING FOR ALL THIS TIME!?
I WASN'T HIDING.
HHHHH

SEE, THAT DIDN'T FEEL BETTER EITHER, DID IT?
AND I WASN'T HIDING.
I WAS IN L.A. THINGS GOT VERY FUNKY. I'M OKAY NOW.
I'M BETTER THAN OKAY.

I DON'T GIVE A CRAP ABOUT L.A.!
WHY DID YOU PUT US THROUGH THIS F$#¢ING HELL FOR THE PAST YEAR!?

YOU FUNDAMENTALLY SHIFTED THE BALANCE OF POWER IN THIS WORLD, BUFFY.
PEOPLE DIE WHEN THAT HAPPENS. EVERY TIME.
IT COULD NEVER BE AS SIMPLE AS YOU HOPED. NOT ON THIS PLANE. BUT IT WAS A PURE ACT, AND IT MEANT YOU WERE READY.

HUFF--!

THE MASK, THE CULT... IT WASN'T JUST TO DISTRACT THE BAD GUYS.
IT WAS TO FOCUS YOU, TOO. TO PUSH YOU TO BE WHAT YOU'VE BECOME.
THAT TWIST IN YOUR BELLY ISN'T JUST RAGE, OR CONFUSION--AND FOR ONCE, IT'S NOT EVEN GUILT.
YOU FEE ME, BUFF YOU FEEL

I'D NEVER TELL HIM HE'S RIGHT.
THERE IS NO "US"!
UT AS HE SAYS THE WORDS--
THERE'S *ALWAYS* BEEN US.
YOU CAN KEEP SWINGING, BUT YOU KNOW I CAN FEEL YOU COMING.
I KNOW HE'S RIGHT.
GET AWAY FROM ME.
Y'SEE THAT ERE? THAT GLOW YOUR ARM EVERY E YOU GET CLOSE?
THIS ISN'T JUST ANOTHER FISTFIGHT, BUFFY.
THIS IS HISTORY.
WHAT WAS THAT?
I DON'T HEAR ANYTHING.
I THINK THEY'RE TALKING.
AND LOOK AT AT--NOW YOUR OW'S STARTING TO EXPAND.
THERE'S NO GLOW.
YOU'RE IMAGINING A GLOW.

BUFFY, LET GO.
FOR ONE MINUTE, LET GO OF WHAT YOU THINK YOU UNDERSTAND, AND LET YOUR BODY TELL YOU THE TRUTH.
MY... BODY...ISN'T TALKING...

IT'S SINGING.
IT'S JOY, BUFFY.
YOU AND I DON'T HAVE A LOT OF EXPERIENCE WITH JOY. BUT I FEEL IT, BEING THIS CLOSE TO YOU, I FEEL A CONNECTION EVEN I WASN'T PREPARED FOR.

FORGET WHAT I SAID ABOUT HISTORY-- THIS ISN'T JUST HISTORY.
THIS IS US, BUFF.
THIS IS OUR FUTURE.

YOU DON'T KNOW ME LIK YOU USED T KNOW ME.

MAYBE I DON'T.
BUT I DO KNOW THERE'S A REASON WE'RE BOTH STANDING HERE, FLUSHED WITH THIS UNHOLY POWER.

THERE'S A REASON I LOVED YOU THE MOMENT I SAW YOU.

THERE'S A REASON WE CAN'T BE HAPPY WITH ANYONE ELSE.

AND THERE'S A ASON YOUR WHOLE ODY IS GLOWING RIGHT NOW.
AND THERE'S A REASON THAT, DESPITE ALL THIS POWER COURSING THROUGH ME, WHAT I FEEL RIGHT NOW IS WEAK.
I'M TERRIFIED YOU'LL GO. YOU'LL LEAVE BEFORE WE HAVE A CHANCE TO EXPLORE WHAT THIS REALLY IS, THIS GLOW.
WHAT IF, JUST ONCE, THE RIGHT THING FOR US TO DO IS ALSO THE MOST WONDERFUL? BUFFY...

...DON'T YOU WANT TO BE HAPPY?

WHAT WAS THAT?
ANOTHER SONIC BOOM.
I THINK THEY'RE F#@%ING.
Next:
Them F#@%i
plus the true histor
of the universe

# TWILIGHT

## CHAPTER THREE: Them F#©%ing (Plus the True History of the Universe)

REUNION KISSES ARE THE BEST.

YOU GET ALL THE AWKWARD ENERGY--

--ALL THE CHAOS--
ARE WE THERE?
YOU SURE THIS IS TWILIGHT'S H.Q.?
THIS IS H.Q.
GILES...!
FAITH'S HURT!
SHE NEEDS HELP!
'MM NOT HURT.
'MM JUST... BLEEDING
A LOT.

--ALL THE SEMI-COMIC FUMBLING--
THAT'S MY SHIELD!
ARE YOU HIGH?
THE SHIELD WAS MY IDEA!
YEAH, GO TELL JOE SIMON THAT!

PLUS ALL THE CONFUSION--
TWILIGHT IS ANGEL?

--THE UNCERTAINTY--
TWILIGHT IS ANGEL?
BEN IS GLORY?

--THE HEAD-NUMBING RUSH THAT YOU REMEMBER FROM THE FIRST TIME YOU KISSED.
"TWILIGHT IS ANGEL?"
OF COURSE HE IS!
OF COURSE HE IS?
IT DOESN'T EVEN MAKE SENSE.

BUT ONCE U FIND YOUR FOOTING--
NO, NO, IT DOES...
THE FORCES AT WORK HERE--
--ARE THE EXACT SAME AS WHEN THEY FIRST MET.
PASSION AND LOVE ARE MORE POTENT MAGICKS THAN YOU THINK.

YOU'RE TALKING MAGIC WITH A K, AREN'T YOU? SCREW MAGIC WITH A K.
BUFFY NEEDS OUR HELP. WE NEED TO FIND THEM.
WILLOW, DO A SPELL.

XAN, I DON'T THINK YOU WANT THAT.
WHAT WHAT?
I DON'T THINK YOU WANT ME TO FIND THEM RIGHT NOW.
TRUST ME ON THIS. WITH THESE TWO BEING APART AS LONG AS THEY HAVE--

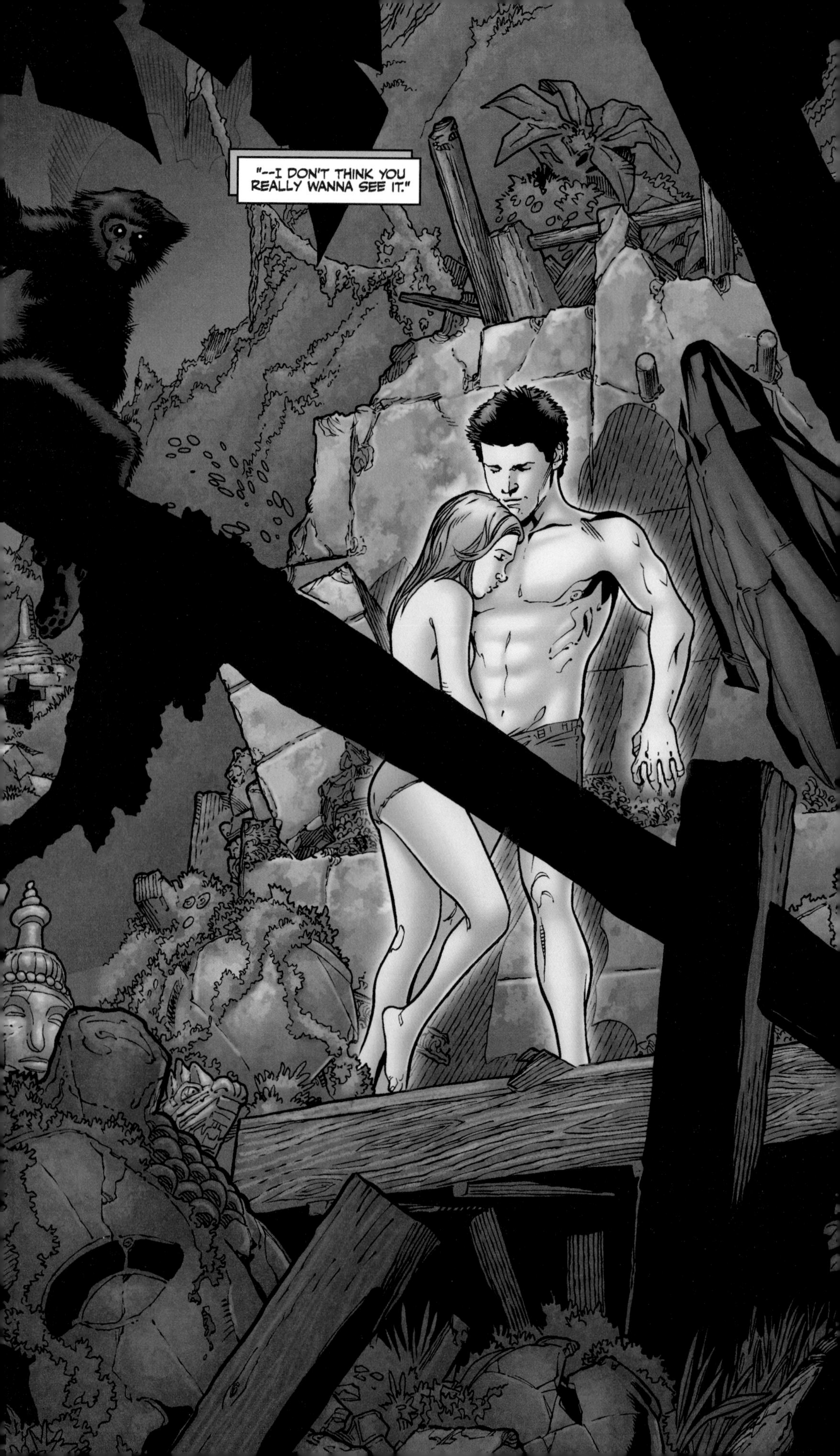
"--I DON'T THINK YOU REALLY WANNA SEE IT."

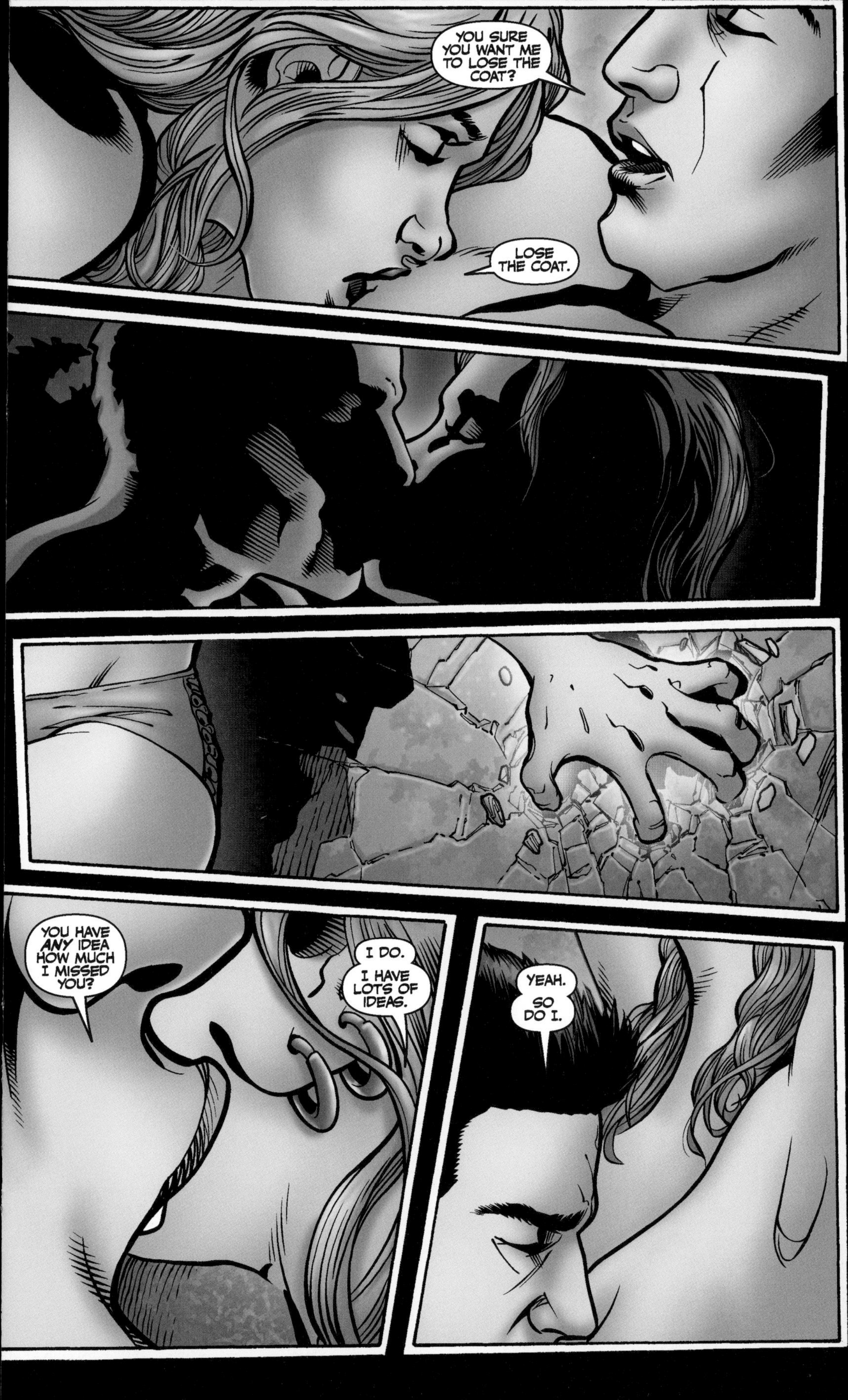
YOU SURE YOU WANT ME TO LOSE THE COAT?
LOSE THE COAT.
YOU HAVE ANY IDEA HOW MUCH I MISSED YOU?
I DO.
I HAVE LOTS OF IDEAS.
YEAH.
SO DO I.

I-I'M NOT BLEEDING ANYMORE.
MY WOUND-- IT'S--
--IT'S GONE.
I'VE GOT SURFACE-WAVE RADAR.
WE CAN FIND THEM ON THAT.
GILES, WHAT THE HELL IS GOING ON?!

DON'T PLAY SILENT TREATMENT!
WITH TWI-- WITH ANGEL...
I HEARD YOU TALKING WITH ANGEL.
DON'T YOU $#%$IN LIE ABOUT IT, G.!

Y-YOU MUST UNDERSTAND--
EVEN AMONG WATCHERS--
THE LAST TIME THEY THOUGHT THIS WAS HAPPENING-- BACK IN THE 1680S--
THIRTY WATCHERS TOOK THEIR OWN LIVES IN FEAR.
GILES, IF YOU KNOW SOMETHING--!
BUT DON'T YOU SEE? NO ONE KNOWS ANYTHING.
IT-IT'S JUST A WATCHER MYTH...A FAIRY TALE.
WE'VE GOT WITCHES, WEREWOLVES AND CENTAURS--
CENTAURETTES!
--THE POINT IS, EVEN WHEN IT COMES TO THE DARK, SCARY ONES...

"--HOW MUCH MORE CAN YOU SHOCK US WITH A FAIRY TALE?"
WANNA TRY IT FLYING?
AFTER.
AFTER WHAT?
AFTER THIS.
FLY UP A LITTLE.

LIKE THIS?
HIGHER.
THERE.
NOW STAY UP THERE.
KEEP YOURSELF WEIGHTLESS AND--

RADAR SAYS THEY'RE NOT MOVING, BUT THEY'RE PICKING UP SPEED, AS IF--

DAWN, YOU'RE IN CHARGE.
I'M DONE.
WAS THAT THEM?
(PLEASE DON'T TELL ME THAT WAS THEM.)
IT'S RUINING EVERYTHING FOR ME.
I GOT MY POWERS BACK.
I'M STRONG AGAIN.
IT'S--IT'S--IT'S EVERYTHING THEY WARNED--
THE UNIVERSE...

THE UNIVERSE IS ANSWERING.
GILES, YOU HAVE *ZERO* SECONDS TO TELL ME WHAT THE HELL THIS HAS TO DO WITH THE UNIVERSE!
THINK OF HOW THE WORLD WORKS...

"NATURE ISN'T WASTEFUL.
"IT DOESN'T PUT ANYTHING IN THE ECOSYSTEM THAT IT DOESN'T NEED.
"IF ONE SIDE FEEDS TOO MUCH, SMALLER ANIMALS LOSE THEIR FOOD AND THE ENTIRE ECOSYSTEM COLLAPSES."
IT'S NO DIFFERENT WITH A SLAYER.
THINK OF WHAT KEEPS THE VAMPIRE POPULATION IN CHECK.
YOU'VE HEARD IT BEFORE, YES...?

"...DEMON BLOOD CREATED THE FIRST VAMPIRES...
"BUT SOON AFTER THE CREATURES APPEARED..."
INTO EVERY GENERATION A SLAYER IS BORN.
"PRECIS
"WHEREVER A VAMPIRE, THERE WOULD ALWAYS BE A SLAYER.
"GENERATION AFTER GENERATION, THE BATTL WOULD BE FOUGHT.

"AND LOST.
KK

"AND LOST AGAIN.
KK

BUT THE BALANCE WOULD ALWAYS BE KEPT."

ACTUALLY, WHEN YOU SAY IT LIKE THAT, IT SOUNDS LIKE A REALLY BAD PLAN.
GUYS, WE'VE GOT CYCLONES REPORTED IN SIX... SEVEN...EIGHT COUNTRIES!
IT IS A REALLY BAD PLAN!
THOUSANDS OF VAMPIRES VERSUS ONE SLAYER?
HOW IS THAT FAIR?

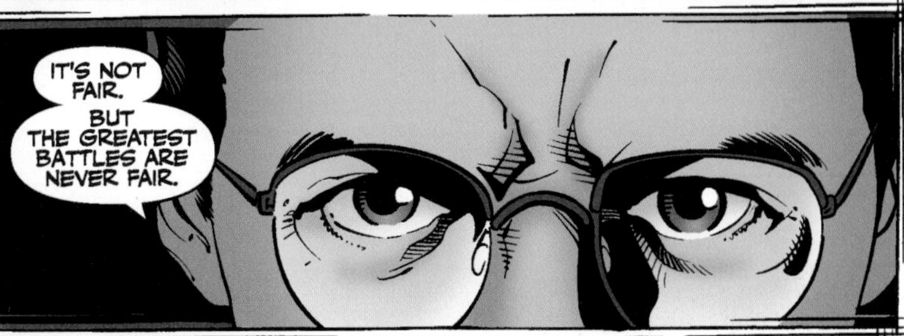
IT'S NOT FAIR.
BUT THE GREATEST BATTLES ARE NEVER FAIR.

"THINK OF THE BALANCE."

EARTH TEMPERATURE JUST WENT UP 0.9 DEGREES IN THE NORTHERN HEMISPHERE.
ROSSBY WAVES--
--WHATEVER THEY ARE--
--ARE CHURNING FOUR PERCENT FASTER IN EVERY OCEAN.

"HOWEVER MUCH BUFFY AND ANGEL MIGHT LOVE OR MISS EACH OTHER--
"--WHAT BUFFY'S EXPERIENCING RIGHT NOW--

"--IS THE PULL OF SOMETHING FAR MORE ANCIENT--"
LUZON, PHILIPPINES.

"--FAR MORE POWERFUL--"
THE INDIAN OCEAN.

"--AND FAR MORE DESTRUCTIV THAN ANYONE IN THIS OMNIVER HAS EVER FELT BEFORE."
THREE DAYS AGO.
IT WAS...LIKE AN AFTERSHOCK.
FALLOUT FROM SOM CATACLYSM MYTHICAL EVENT.
"IF THE UNIVERSE IS SMART ENC TO CREATE VAMPIRES AND SLAY TO BALANCE EACH OTHER OU

"--ISN'T IT ALSO POSSIBLE THAT, WELL--

"--THAT THE UNIVERSE IS ALSO SMART ENOUGH TO HAVE A FAR BIGGER PLAN FOR THEM?"
FUH

FUH
DO.

NOT.
F%#$ING.
STOP.

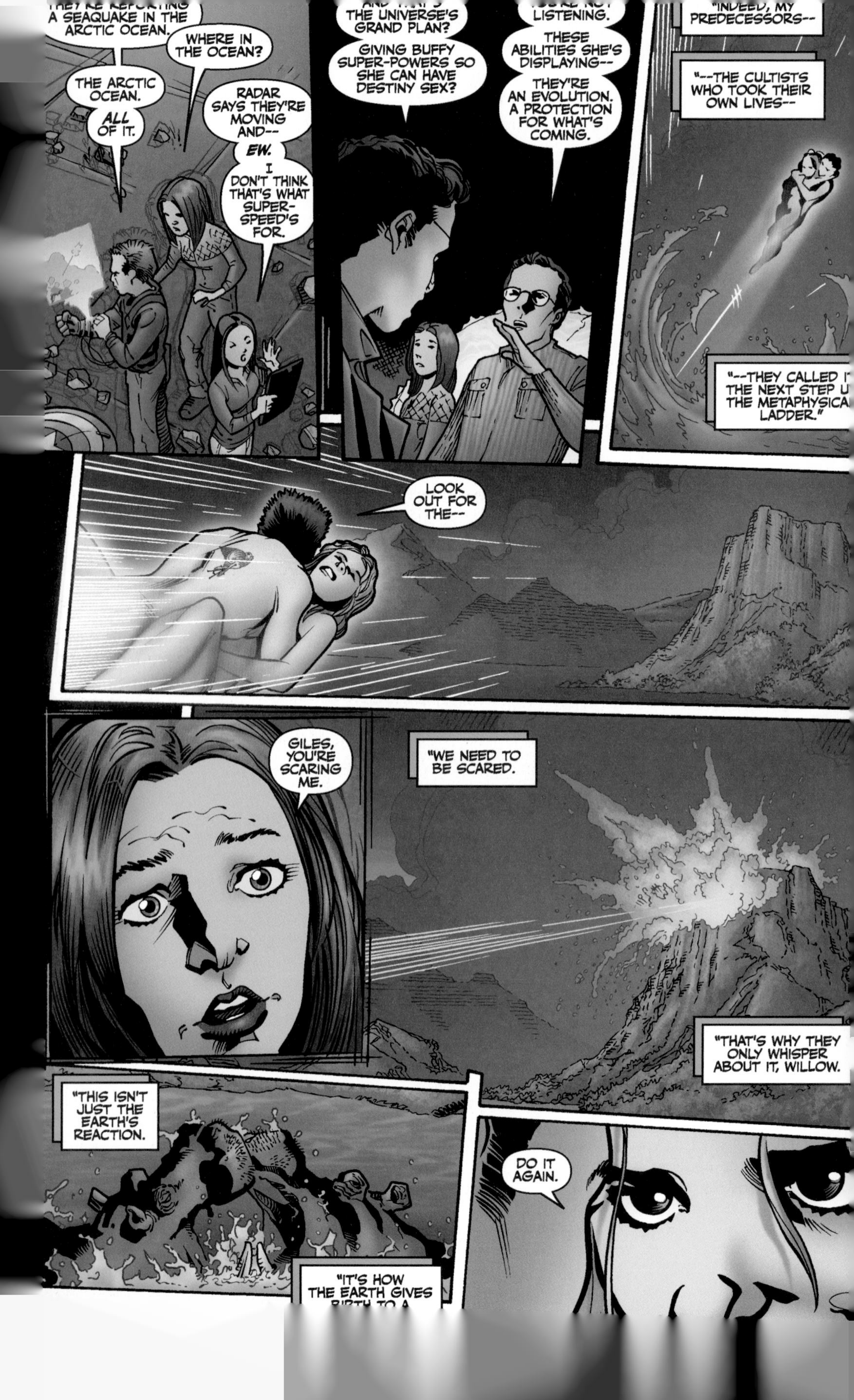

A SEAQUAKE IN THE ARCTIC OCEAN.
WHERE IN THE OCEAN?
THE ARCTIC OCEAN. ALL OF IT.
RADAR SAYS THEY'RE MOVING AND-- EW.
I DON'T THINK THAT'S WHAT SUPER-SPEED'S FOR.
THE UNIVERSE'S GRAND PLAN?
GIVING BUFFY SUPER-POWERS SO SHE CAN HAVE DESTINY SEX?
LISTENING.
THESE ABILITIES SHE'S DISPLAYING--
THEY'RE AN EVOLUTION. A PROTECTION FOR WHAT'S COMING.
"INDEED, MY PREDECESSORS--
"--THE CULTISTS WHO TOOK THEIR OWN LIVES--
"--THEY CALLED I THE NEXT STEP U THE METAPHYSICA LADDER."
LOOK OUT FOR THE--
GILES, YOU'RE SCARING ME.
"WE NEED TO BE SCARED.
"THAT'S WHY THEY ONLY WHISPER ABOUT IT, WILLOW.
"THIS ISN'T JUST THE EARTH'S REACTION.
"IT'S HOW THE EARTH GIVES
DO IT AGAIN.

FOR THOUSANDS OF YEARS, THE UNIVERSE HAS BEEN WATCHING--WAITING TO FIND ONE SLAYER--
"--JUST ONE--
"--WHO MEASURES UP TO ITS TEST.
"CENTURY AFTER CENTURY, THEY ALL MEET THE SAME FATE."
GLOBAL TEMPERATURE IS NOW UP 1.2 DEGREES!
GUYS, WE'VE GOT HURRICANES STARTING!
CAN YOU FEEL IT?
THE QUAKING...THE RUMBLING--
IT'S COMING...
"UNTIL BUFFY SUMMERS CAME ALONG AND DID THE ONE THING THAT NO SLAYER--NO SLAYER IN HISTORY--HAD EVER DONE BEFORE."
SHE SHARED THE POWER.
"SHE DIDN'T JUST SHARE IT, WILLOW.
"WITH YOU, AND THE POWER OF THE SCYTHE, SHE CREATED IT.
"SHE GAVE THIS WORLD A NEW BREED. A NEW EVOLUTION.

"AND THIS IS THE UNIVERSE'S REWARD.
"THE POWER THAT WILL LET HER REACH THE NEXT STEP ON THE LADDER--
"THE POWER TO SURVIVE THE TWILIGHT."
THAT'S FINE, BUT WHAT ABOUT ANGEL?
NO OFFENSE---
(AND BY THE WAY, I HATE YOU ALL)
--BUT WHY'S ANGEL GET A REWARD?
BECAUSE HE'S THE YIN TO HER YANG.
NOW THERE'S
FANTASY
IT'S NOT A FANTASY. EVERYONE KNOWS IT.
GILES SAID THE UNIVERSE WAS SMART.
SO THINK HOW SMART IT'S BEING--
"ANGEL'S THE PIECE WE WERE MISSING.
"SURE, BUFFY SHARED HER POWER, BUT WHEN IT COMES TO HER PLACE IN THE SLAYER HISTORY BOOKS--
"--I'M PRETTY SURE THAT'S NOT THE ONLY THING SHE WAS THE FIRST TO DO."

I CAN'T FIND THEM ON RADAR ANYMORE.
THEY'RE MOVING TOO FAST.
I CHECKED.
THEY'RE NOT ON THIS PLANE OF EXISTENCE.
I THINK--
JUH--
JUH--

DON'T ASK ME HOW, BUT--
CAN THEY BE MOVING THROUGH TIME?
JUH--
JUST LIKE THAT...

SOON.

THREE DAYS AGO.

NOW.
OH, GODDESS...
WHAT?
THINK ABOUT IT. SHE SHOULD BE STAKING HIM RIGHT NOW. SHE DID IT ONCE, TO SAVE THE WORLD.
NOW THE WORLD WON'T LET HER.
IT ISN'T JUST REACTING TO WHAT THEY'RE DOING... IT'S URGING THEM ON.

CENTURY.
"IT'S ALL PART OF IT. WHAT'S BEEN, WHAT'S TO COME--OR MIGHT NOT COME...
"THINK OF BUFFY'S TRUEST LOVES.
"VAMPIRES--HUMANS INFECTED BY DEMONS.
"JUST LIKE SLAYERS."
JUST LIKE THAT...!
"BUFFY'S MEANT TO MAKE THAT CONNECTION.
"THAT'S THE UNIVERSE'S GRAND PLAN."
YES.
THEY ARE THE BEST OF THEIR KIND... THE FIRST OF A NEW KIND. AND WHEN THEY TRULY BECOME?
WE HUMANS WON'T MATTER AT ALL.

"AND DO YOU UNDERSTAND HOW QUICKLY THE ANCIENT DEMONS AND MAGICKS WILL COME POURING BACK IN?"
"WARREN, YOU SEEING THAT--!?"
--I'M SHOWING A DIMENSIONAL RIFT--
HEY, PEOPLE-I-WANT-TO-KILL! IT'S RAINING DEMONS!
GILES, WHEN YOU WER TALKING WITH ANGEL--
HE SAID... IN GERMANY... ENGLAND--
HE SAID YOU WERE SEARCHING FO SOMETHING.
I-I WAS--
THERE ARE RUMORS OF A TOTEM--
--AN ITEM THAT COULD STOP THEM IF THEY GREW TOO POWERFUL.
I KNOW IT SOUNDS HORRIBLE, BUT THAT'S WHAT I WAS SEARCHING FOR--
"I NEEDED TO KNOW HOW TO KILL A GOD.
"BUT LOOK AROUND.
"IT'S TOO LATE NOW--
"TWILIGHT IS HERE!"

WHUH...
TH-THAT WAS--
SPRINKLES.
UM.
WHERE ARE WE?
(AND WHY'M DRESSED?)
BUFF...DID YOU--?
HOW'D WE--?
WAIT.
IS THIS--? IT IS, ISN'T IT?
IT TOOK THE TWO OF US--
ANGEL.
ENGLISH.
PLEASE.
DON'T YOU SEE? TO-- IF WE PIERCED THE FINAL WALL--
THE KEYS WERE *US!*
THE KEYS TO *WHAT?*
TO EVERYTHING.
LOOK AROUND.
THEY SAID IT DIDN'T EXIST.
BUT IT DOES. IT ALWAYS HAS.
AND NOW IT'S OURS.
HERE WE ARE, BUFFY.

WELCOME TO TWILIGHT.
Next: The Power of Love

# TWILIGHT

## The Final Chapter: The Power of Love

IT'S NOT A TRAP.
IT'S ALWAYS A TRAP.
THAT'S HOW IT IS--
WE GET ONE MOMENT OF PEACE--
THAT WAS WAY MORE THAN PEACE. YOUR FINGER WAS--
DO NOT TALK ABOUT IT YE WE'RE NOT TALKIN ABOUT IT YET.
THE POINT IS, THAT'S--
--THAT'S OUR LIVES
WE CATCH OUR BREATH, WE TURN AROUND--
--AND JU AS WE FIG OUT WHERE TRANSPOR US...
"--THE VICIOUS ORCS COME OVER THE MOUNTAIN."
LISTEN.
THEY'RE COMING.

NO.
YOU'RE WRONG, BUFFY.
THE ORCS AREN'T COMING.
BUT--
--THAT'S NOT--
THE ORCS *ALWAYS* COME.
UNTIL THE DAY THEY DON'T.

NO--THE MOMENT YOU LOOK AWAY--
THE BAD GUY JUMPS OUT...
THERE'S A BOMB UNDER THE CAR...
THE APPLE'S BEEN POISONED...

APPLE, MAYBE. POISON, NO.
WELL, SOMETHING WAS IN THAT APPLE, 'CAUSE WHAT I'M FEELING IS A WHOLE LOT WEIRDER THAN "AFTERGLOW."
WHICH I AM ALSO FEELING.

HAVE YOU NOTICED OUR CLOTHES ARE CHANGING?

NOT TO MENTION--BUFFY, LOOK--THE WORLD.
I THINK WE'RE IN--

TWILIGHT!?
WAIT. SO ILIGHT'S A PLACE?
YOU MUST UNDERSTAND--
WHAT I UNDERSTAND IS THAT YOU KNEW ABOUT THIS. GODDESS, BEFORE YOU EVEN MET BUFFY, YOU KNEW!
IT WAS A MYTH.
AN UNPROVABLE YPOTHESIS BASED ON THEORIES THAT SEEK TO EXPLAIN THE BEGINNING OF TIME.
I DON'T WANNA TALK ABOUT RELIGION, GILES!
I WANNA KNOW WHY ANGEL DRESSED LIKE A FETISH BAD GUY AND BECAME A KILLER!
FAIR QUESTION...
I'M NOT RE "KILLER" THE RIGHT WORD.
HE POWER AT TWILIGHT AS ON ITS UBJECTS--
YOU KNOW WHAT, FORGET IT. JUST TELL ME WHY WE'RE BEING ATTACKED!
IS THIS STILL PART OF THE UNIVERSE'S BALANCE?
THERE IS NO BALANCE. NOT ANYMORE.
WHEN BUFFY AND ANGEL ASCENDED--
IN NAUGHTY FASHION...
--THEY WERE BREACHED INTO A NEW REALITY.
AND THERE IS NO BIRTH WITHOUT BLOOD.
SO THESE DEMONS POURING OUT ALL OVER US ARE SOME SORT OF AFTERBIRTH?
WAIT! "PLACENTURIANS"! THAT I'M GONNA COPYRIGHT.
YOU'RE CLOSER THAN YOU KNOW.
WHEN YOU'RE BORN INTO THE WORLD, YOU VACATE THE OLD ONE. IT BECOMES...

--UTTERLY EXPENDABLE.
WE'VE GOT FIVE DIFFERENT TEARS IN REALITY--
SIX!
NEW ONE OVER BURMA!
SIX, THEN.
THOUGH... BURMA?
Y'HEAR ME, XANDER?
"IT'S POURING DEMONS!"
KENNEDY, NOTIFY ALL OUR TEAMS! GLOBALLY!
I WANT THEM IN HOLDING PATTERNS NEAR WHATEVER ENTRY POINT THEY'RE CLOSEST TO!
ALREADY ON IT.
UGLIES ARE HERE!
YOU HEARD HER, PEOPLE!

GRAB WHATEVER WEAPONS YOU CAN FIND!
I WANT THE SHIELD!
NO DEAL.
YOU CAN HAVE THE REPULSORS.
AND F.Y.I.-- THE SHIELD DOESN'T BOOMERANG BACK LIKE YOU THINK.
THEN WHY DO YOU WANT IT SO BAD?
WHY DO YOU THINK?
WARREN, LOOK OUT!

ANDREW, YOU OKAY?
ANDREW...?
KUUUNG
XANDER! WILLOW!
ANDREW'S BLEEDING BAD!
REPULSOR SHIELD AT 94%
WARREN DOES KNOW WE'RE GOING TO KILL THEM AFTER ALL THIS, DOESN'T HE?
RELAX, AMY.
CURRENT PROBLEMS FIRST.
OUR ERSTWHILE LEADER AND HIS COOZE ARE AWOL, AND IF I WERE GUESSING--

'D BET THAT
HAS NO IDEA
AT HE JUST
'PED OPEN."
BUT WE DID HAVE THE SEX PART, RIGHT?
YES, WE HAD THE SEX PART.
MOTHER OF MERCY, WE HAD THE SEX PART.
GOOD, BECAUSE QUITE HONESTLY, I'M TILL FEELING...WELL... SATISFIED--
--AND I WANNA T MAKE SURE WE'RE SOMEHOW STANDING N MY MIND, OR IN SOME 1 WHERE I'M THE SNOW-OBE AT THE END OF ST. ELSEWHERE.

SO MUCH DOUBT. ALWAYS.
IT IS YOUR MIND, BUFFY--IT'S BOTH OF OURS--BUT WE'RE NOT TRAPPED IN IT.
I THINK WE'RE FINALLY FREE.

YOU DON'T EVEN KNOW, DO YOU?
YOU'RE GUESSING AS MUCH AS I AM, TWILIGHT.

YOU KNOW THAT'S NOT WHAT I AM.
THINK OF HOW WE GOT HERE.
THIS PLACE--
--IT'S A PLACE OF PLEASURE--
--A PLACE YOU'VE NEVER BEEN--
--AND THE ONLY WAY WE GET HERE IS WITH EACH OTHER.

ONE, THAT IS THE SINGLE VELVEETA CHEESIEST COME-ON LINE I'VE EVER HEARD.
TWO, IF YOU SAY THIS IS HEAVEN OR SOMETHING STUPID LIKE THAT, I WILL SOCK YOU.

I KNOW WHY YOU USE THE JOKES, BUFFY.
IT'S THE SAME REASON XANDER DOES.
THAT'S NOT TRUE. XANDER ENJOYS HIS JOKES.

AND YOU CAN MAKE AS MANY AS YOU WANT.
BUT IT DOESN'T CHANGE WHERE WE ARE.

LOOK AROUND...
YOU SEE IT, DON'T YOU?

THIS PLACE--
IT REACTS TO US.

THEN WHY'S IT KEEP
TING ME IN GRADUATION GOWNS?
NO ONE
OKS GOOD
RADUATION GOWNS.
THAT'S NOT A GRADUATION GOWN.
IT'S A SPANISH MOURNING ROBE FROM THE SIXTEENTH CENTURY--

"--WORN BY A SLAYER FROM THE LATE 1590S."

JR OUTFIT
BEFORE
THAT--
--THE INDIAN SARI--
--WAS FROM A SLAYER IN THE SEVENTEENTH CENTURY.
I KNOW YOU FEEL IT, BUFFY.
THIS PLACE--
THINK OF IT AS A HIGHER PLANE--

IT'S *NOT* A HIGHER PLANE.
IT'S LIKE I SAID.
*IT'S A TRAP.*

BOTH OF THOSE
STATEMENTS CAN BE TRUE.
WILL YOU STOP TALKING LIKE GILES?

SEE?
IT'S NOT A HIGHER PLANE!
IT'S A DAFFY DUCK CARTOON!

THAT'S THE BEAUTY OF IT.
JUST LIKE WE--
IT LOOKS THAT WAY BECAUSE YOU MADE IT THAT WAY.
OH.
I GET IT.
THAT'S WHY IT FIRST LOOKED LIKE EDEN.

IT'S THE ONE THING THE BEST PHILOSOPHERS HAD RIGHT.
WE BUILD IT OURSELVES, BUFFY.
PARADISE IS OURS TO WRITE.

THAT'S FINE.
GREAT SPEECH.
BUT ALL I WANNA WRITE IS THE PART WHERE I SEE MY FRIENDS.
YOU KNO WHERE T ARE.
THEY'R WHEREV YOU WA THEM BE.

WELL THEN I WANT THEM TO BE RIGHT--

OOOH.
THAT WAS ACTUALLY EASIER THAN I THOUGHT.

ELL THAT'S RTAINLY THE CK PART OF EDEN.
DID E CAUSE THAT?
I-I DIDN'T THINK IT WOULD BE...
WE CAN HELP THEM. WE CAN FIX IT.
WE CAN FIX *EVERYTHING,* BUFFY.

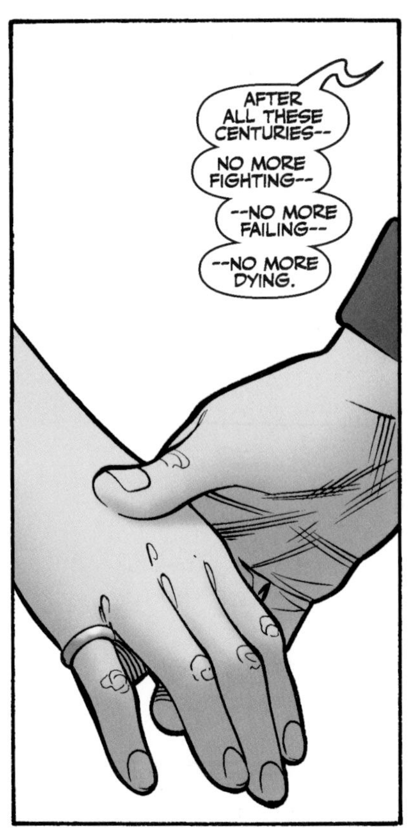
AFTER ALL THESE CENTURIES--
NO MORE FIGHTING--
--NO MORE FAILING--
--NO MORE DYING.

THE UNIVERSE WE'RE GOING TO MAKE...
IT'S NOT JUST THAT WE GET TO BE *TOGETHER,* BUFFY--

--WE FINALLY GET TO BE HAPPY.

FAITH!
I GOT ANDREW!
YOU'RE BLEEDING.
YOUR POWERS ARE BACK, BUT YOU'RE BLEEDING...
THESE PAN-DIMENSIC F@%$ERS AIN'T LIK ANYTHING WE'VE SE
EVEN WITH THEIR POWERS BA OUR GIRLS ARE GO GET SLAUGHTERE OUT THERE.
WILLOW!
STOP YELLING PEOPLE'S NAMES, XANDER!
WE'RE TRYING OUR BEST!
ANOTHER CONTAINMENT SPELL?
THEY BROKE THROUGH FOUR ALREADY.
TELEPORTING?
US OR THEM?
EITHER. ANYTHING.
JUST GET US OUT OF HERE BEFORE THEY--
WHUMP
ARE YOU THE MAGES?
YOU SMELL OF BOTH GOOD AND EVIL.
MIND YOUR MANNERS.

CAN HANDLE
BUFFY.
YOU
KNOW THAT.
IT'S NO DIFFERENT THAN WHEN YOU DIED.
THEY'LL SURVIVE. THEY ALWAYS DO.

YOU'RE JUST SAYING THAT BECAUSE YOU CAN LIVE WITHOUT KNOWING THE OUTCOME.
I CAN'T.
THE OUTCOME IS BEYOND US.
THE ONLY ABSOLUTE IN THE EARTH IS THAT IT WILL END.

BUT TODAY IS DIFFERENT THAN LATER.
MY FRIENDS ARE DIFFERENT THAN--ARE YOU REALLY NOT GETTING THIS?

THAT'S WHAT I NEED TO FIGHT FOR. NOT HAPPINESS. NOT HUMANITY.
THEM.
THOSE PEOPLE.

YOU ARE FIGHTING FOR THEM.
THAT'S WHY YOU WERE SEN HERE!
THIS IS THE END.

"THE END OF WHAT'S DOWN THERE--
"AND THE BEGI OF A NEW ER
THE BEGINNING OF US.

DON'T
/E TO
OOSE.
THE UNIVERSE ALREADY CHOSE US!
ALL WE HAVE TO DO IS LEAVE BEHIND THE LOWER PLANE.
LEAVE BEHIND?
MY FAMILY IS ON THAT LOWER PLANE.

"MY FAMILY."
BUFFY...!
SHE CAN'T HEAR YOU.
SHE CAN.
SHE ALWAYS CAN.

YOU DO UNDERSTAND
AT BEING HERE
WHAT YOU'RE MEANT FOR?
DON'T YOU KNOW ME BY NOW, ANGEL?

I NEVER DO WHAT I'M MEANT FOR.

RRRRP

IF YOU STAY HERE, WE CAN EVOLVE.
F#*% EVOLUTION.

SO YOU'LL JUST WALK AWAY AND IGNORE WHAT THE UNIVERSE HAS SPENT MILLIONS OF YEARS SETTING IN MOTION?

YUP.

OKAY.
LET'S GO.

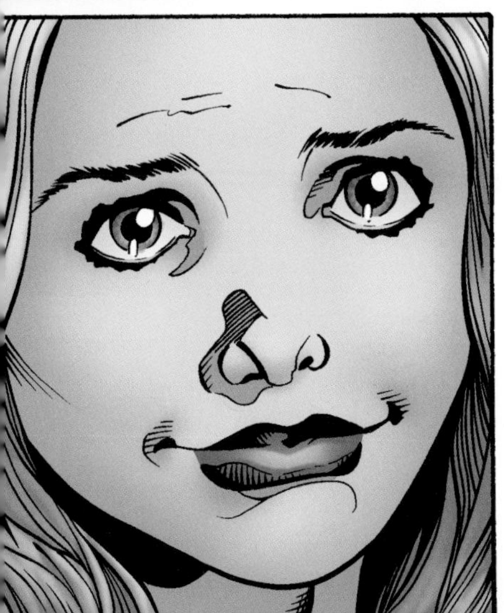

I DID MISS YOU.
I MISSED YOU TOO.

I'LL TAKE THE ONES ON THE LEFT.
THEN I GET THE ONES ON THE RIGHT.

BUFFY!
BUFFY!

BUFFY!

AND...TWILIGHT.
CAN I JUST MENTION THAT I PREFERRED ANGELUS?
HAD THAT COMING...
WHAT YOU GOT COMING YOU BETTER HOPE NEVER COMES. GO SLAY.
HOW MANY OF THESE THINGS ARE THERE?
UH, INFINITY-ISH?
WILLOW, I'M SORRY...
I KNOW, I KNOW--YOU DON'T KNOW WHAT CAME ALL OVER YOU.

WE'VE GOT ANOTHER ATTACK COMING!
THEY'VE GOT A WEAPON ON THIS ONE!
I SEE IT!
THAT'S NOT A WEAPON!
THAT'S--
OH, THIS IS GONNA BE GOOD.
RRRRRMBLE

IS THAT--?
OH, THIS IS GONNA BE BAD.
ENOUGH OF THIS.
YOU WANNA PUT THESE DEMONS DOWN AND END THIS "TWILIGHT" CRAP ONCE AND FOR ALL?

...YOU TALK TO *ME.*

# WILLOW: GODDESSES AND MONSTERS

Script JOSS WHEDON

Pencils KARL MOLINE

Inks ANDY OWENS

Colors MICHELLE MADSEN

Letters RICHARD STARKINGS &
COMICRAFT'S JIMMY BETANCOURT

*This story takes place before the events of*
Buffy the Vampire Slayer *Season Eight.*

GODDESSES & MONSTERS

THE JOURNEY BEGINS...
...AND ALREADY I'M OUT OF MY DEPTH.
GODDESS...
IT'S... SO...

...DERIVATIVE.
TRACK 9.33
F$%&ING WIZARD SCHOOL, IT'S ALL THE RAGE.
I MEAN, IT'S COOL BY ME. I HA
HUNDRED YEARS OF FALLING DO
A RABBIT HOLE AND S#&% THA
SAID "DRINK ME," SO THIS IS STILL FRESH.
BUT... ISN'T THIS...

10642
IT DOES SEEM KINDA THEME-PARKY.
WE'RE SCRATCHING THE SURFACE. THE ENTRYWAY TO A BOSS FLOAT IS ALWAYS CULLED FROM COLLECTIVE CONSCIOUSNESS. SOFTENS THE BLOW.
THERE'S GONNA BE A BLOW?
FOR A LADY THAT ALMOST ENDED THE WORLD, YOU'RE KIND OF A PUSS.
OH, I NEVER --
COME ON. TIME TO CATCH THE TRAIN.

THIS ISN'T A TRAIN.
WOW, ARE YOU EVER A DYKE.

THAT TERM IS OFFENSIVE.
OR MAYBE IT'S EMPOWERING -- I CAN'T ALWAYS KEEP UP. HOW'D YOU KNOW?

THE FIELD, THE OPENI PETALS...WITH STRAIG WICS, IT'S A FOREST. TA THRUSTING TREES..
THE SECOND LEVEL IS YOU, BUT IT'S STILL SURFACE.
BEING A FIERCE 'MO HAS NOTHING TO DO WITH YOUR POWER. THIS IS YO RELATING TO THE OUTSIDE WORLD.

WE'RE GOING DEEPER THAN THAT.

AH!
VERY LITERAL!
RELAX.

BUT ALSO TAKE A RIDICULOUSLY DEEP BREATH.

YOU'RE NOT ACTUALLY BREATHING ON THIS PLANE, BUT YOU CAN STILL SUFFOCATE.
ESPECIALLY IF YOU THINK ABOUT SUFFOCATING, OR IF SOMEONE SAYS THE WORD "SUFFOCATE."
LIKE, "SUFFOCATE SUFFOCATE YOU'RE GONNA SUFFOCATE."

THAT'S ENOUGH, MUFFITT...

I'LL TAKE HER FROM HERE.

three days earlier

ARE YOU SURE ABOUT THIS?
"SURE" WOULD BE OVERSTATING IT.
IT'S JUST... IT'S KIND OF A TRADITION.

AND WE'RE TRADITIONAL SINCE WHEN NOW?
IT'S PART OF A WITCH'S PATH. A PART I SKIPPED OVER.

'CAUSE YOU'RE A GODDESS.
NOT EVEN.
AND GODDESSES DON'T LEAVE THEIR GIRLFRIENDS ALL ALONE TO TAKE REMEDIAL MAGIC IN SOME WEIRD DIMENSION THAT PROBABLY HAS ZERO CELL-PHONE RECEPTION.
KEN DOLL...

PET NAMES
WHILE I'M
OUTING.
SEE ABOVE RE:
GODDESS.
I
HAVE CRAZY
POWER.
POWER
IS NOT
KNOWLEDGE.
IN A WAY, IT'S
ALMOST THE
OPPOSITE.

LOOK AT THESE GIRLS.
A FEW MONTHS AGO THEY
BECAME SLAYERS.
I WAS ONE OF THEM,
WILLPOWER.
NO PET
NAMES WHILE I'M
LECTURING.
ALSO
THAT ONE'S MORE
OR LESS LAME.

THESE GIRLS WEREN'T
IN THE GAME LIKE YOU.
THEY DIDN'T KNOW
WHICH END WAS UP.
NOW
THEY HAVE
YOU.

DID NOT ASK
TO BE A DRILL
SERGEANT--
BUT YOU'RE A
GOOD ONE.
THEY NEED IT,
AND THEY'LL KEEP
YOU OCCUPIED WHILE
I'M AWAY.

WELL, THE BLONDE WITH
THE R. CRUMB THIGHS
COULD PROBABLY KEEP
ME OCCUPIED...
I COULD
TURN YOU INTO
A NEWT. FOR
REALSIES.

MAN, I JUST MASTERED
MONOGAMY, NOW
I HAVE TO PRACTICE
NOT-GETTING-ANY-
AT-ALLGAMY.
YOU'RE
A HARSH
MISTRESS.
JUST
DON'T FORGET
ABOUT ME.

"FORGET ABOUT HER."

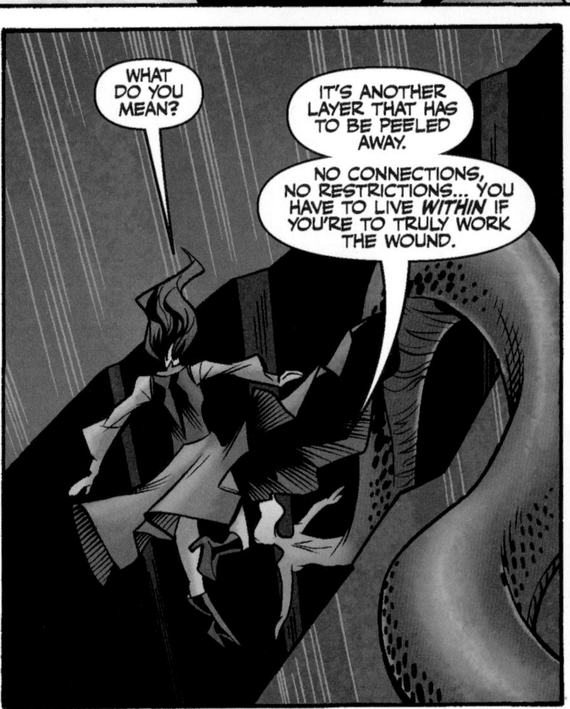
WHAT DO YOU MEAN?
IT'S ANOTHER LAYER THAT HAS TO BE PEELED AWAY.
NO CONNECTIONS, NO RESTRICTIONS... YOU HAVE TO LIVE *WITHIN* IF YOU'RE TO TRULY WORK THE WOUND.

WOUND?
I THOUGHT THE FLOATABOUT WAS JUST NORMAL WICCY TRAINING? NOBODY SAID ANYTHING ABOUT...
I HAVE A WOUND?

YOU HAVE A PART OF IT.
SO CLARITY NOT THE CATCH OF THE DAY, HUH?
RELAX.

THE DARKNESS WILL ILLUMINATE.
CAN I HAVE WHEELY-GIRL BACK?

STOP!

NOT THIS ONE. NOT THIS TAINTED WRETCH.
IT'S VERY NICE TO DON'T MACE ME.

HY DON'T E CALM DOWN, LOVE...
ALUWYN, ARE YOU MAD? YOU KNOW WHO THIS IS!
YOU DO? DO I?

THE PATH IS NOT RESERVED FOR THE RIGHTEOUS.
WE BOTH KNOW WHERE THIS LEADS.
AND I WOULD BE WHO NOW?

WHAT WE KNOW IS THAT NOTHING IS SET. WITH THE RIGHT GUIDE--
YOU? ALUWYN, YOU ARE SAGA VASUKI--YOU THRIVE ON CHAOS. YOU'D LOVE TO SEE HER CORRUPTED.
AND I WOULD KNOW ME FROM...?

ALUWYN, YOU KNOW I LOVE YOU BECAUSE OF THAT SPELL YOU DID THAT TIME, BUT I STAND WITH THE FORCES OF ORDER.
SHE TURNS BACK OR SHE DIES.

ALWAYS BLACK-AND-WHITE THINKING WITH THESE DEMIGODS. "ORDER." "CHAOS." AS IF THEY AREN'T INTERTWINED LIKE LOVERS. AS IF THE UNIVERSES DON'T DEPEND ON BOTH.

ALL RIGHT THEN. A FIGHT TO THE DEATH.

WHOA! WAIT... WHY CAN'T WE BE FRIENDS? GIVE PEACE A CHANCE, 'KAY? WE CAN WORK IT OUT!

STOP! IN THE NAME OF LOVE!

YOU HAVE TO FIGHT BACK, CHILD.
WHY? AND WHY CAN I ONLY SPEAK LIKE OLD-PERSON RADIO?
I BELIEVE I CAN FLY!

YOU HAVEN'T LET GO OF THE SURFACE, AND IT'S CAUGHT YOU IN A LOOP.

IT'S A STUPID LOOP!
DO YOU **REALLY** WANNA HURT ME?

CAN'T YOU UNDERSTAND WHAT A THREAT YOU POSE? CARE YOU NOTHING FOR YOUR WORLD?

DON'T GO BREAKING MY HEART.

DHUUMMmmm
YOU DIDN'T KILL HIM.
I'M NOT A KILLER.
WAIT! IS THAT A SONG? THAT'S NOT A SONG!
YOUR PANIC HAS PASSED. AND YOU MET YOUR FIRST REAL CHALLENGE.
I DIDN'T PUT A SPELL ON HIM, BY THE WAY.
HE JUST HAD TROUBLE WITH HIS FEELINGS.
YEAH, WELL...
LOVE IS A BATTLEFIELD.

AND NOW WE GO ON A BOAT.
THEY *SAID* YOU WERE SPECIAL...

YEAH.
NO THANKS.

YOU'LL NEVER FINISH THE JOURNEY IF YOU'RE AFRAID TO GET WET.

THAT'S NOT THE JOURNEY.

YOU ALL KEEP TELLING ME TO GET BEYOND THE SURFACE. THEN YOU TOSS CLICHÉS AT ME.
THE BLACK KNIGHT, THE SEA VOYAGE...THIS ISN'T MY PATH, IS IT?
THIS ISN'T MY PATH AND YOU'RE NOT MY GUIDE.

WELL, SHE GOT THERE SOONER THAN MOST...
SO MANY GET HUNG UP ON THE IDEA THAT SPACE AND TIME HAVE RULES OUT HERE.
SHAME ON YOU, ALUWYN.
SLITHER BACK TO YOUR MAD REALM AND LEAVE THIS WITCH HER REASON.
WHO IS MY GUIDE, THEN?
DO I HAVE ONE?

AND ALUWYN... SHE'D RUN YOU IN CIRCLES FOR YEARS JUST FOR THE COMPANY.
WELL, THERE ARE MANY GUIDES ON THE PATH TO WISDOM...
...BUT YOU DO HAVE ONE IN MIND.

TARA...

NO.

NO THANK YOU.

BUT, YOU CHOSE...
I WANTED. I HOPED.

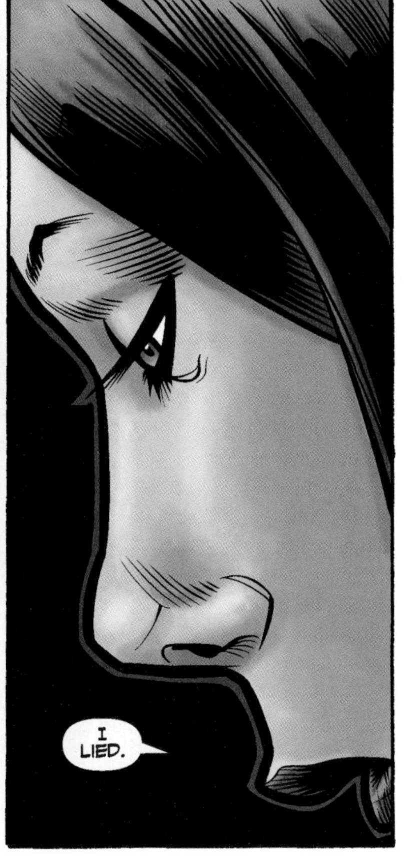
I LIED.

I SAID I WANTED TO UNDERSTAND MY POWER--
--AND I DO.

BUT UNDER THAT, I WANTED TO KNOW MY FATE.
DARKNESS? ENLIGHTENMENT? WAS I A GOOD WITCH, OR A BAD WITCH? I FEEL THE PULL OF EACH. THAT WAS MY SECRET MOTIVE...
BUT IT'S NOT.

UNDER THE UNDER, I JUST WANTED HER.

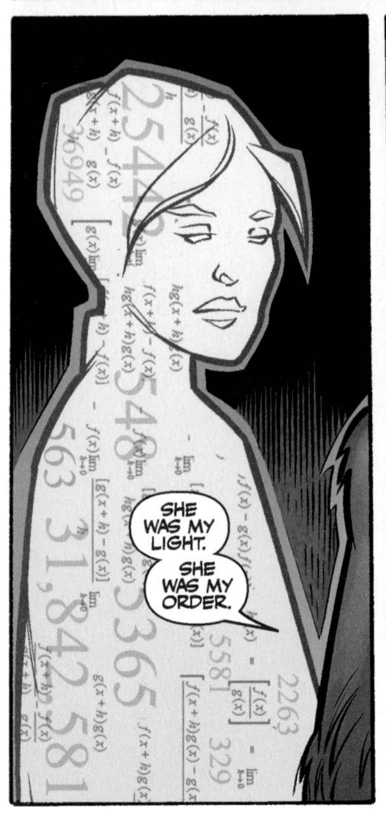
SHE WAS MY LIGHT.
SHE WAS MY ORDER.

SHE WAS MY JOURNEY.

COMPLETED.

BUT EITHER SHE'S AN ILLUSION...
...OR TARA IS AT PEACE.

AND EITHER WAY, NO THANKS.

BWAHHH!!!
SHE ALWAYS GETS LIKE THIS.
I KNOW--EVERYONE ASSUMES IT'S GONNA BE ME.

YOU STILL HAVE TO CHOOSE A GUIDE, YOU KNOW.
THE JOURNEY MAY NOT BE SPATIAL, OR TEMPORAL, BUT THAT DOESN'T MEAN IT'S NOT TREACHEROUS.

WE HAVE MANY TRUSTED FRIENDS IN THIS REALM.
OH FOR THE LOVE OF LIFE STOP SNIFFLING.
SNIFF.

I WILL NEED A GUIDE.
I HAVE SOMEONE IN MIND.
MORONS! ALL OF YOU.
YOU PUT HER ON EDGE! AND GNOG...
DON'T LAY THIS ON US...

THAT "NONE SHALL PASS" ROUTINE MIGHT INTIMIDATE A SCHOOLGIRL.
SHE LOOKED LIKE A SCHOOLGIRL...

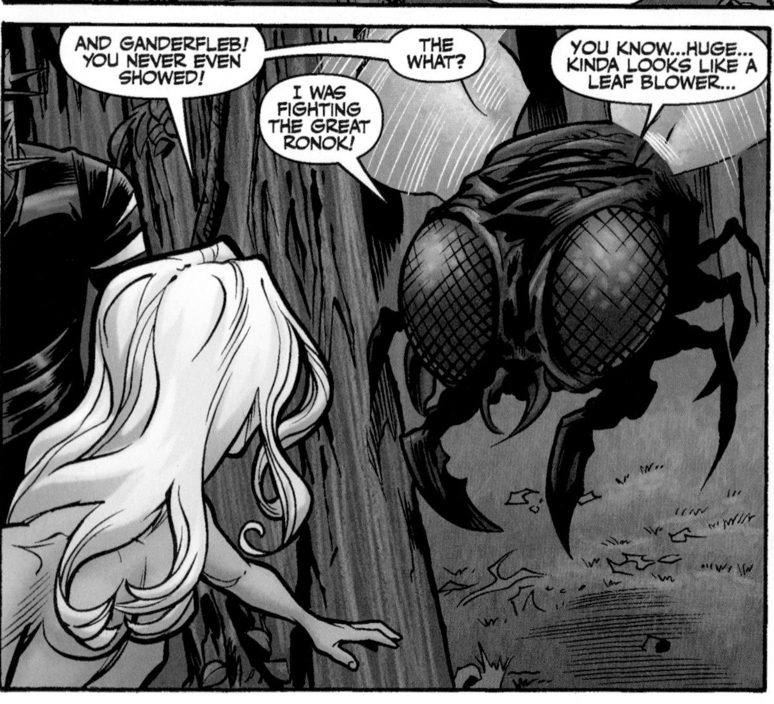
AND GANDERFLEB! YOU NEVER EVEN SHOWED!
THE WHAT?
I WAS FIGHTING THE GREAT RONOK!
YOU KNOW...HUGE... KINDA LOOKS LIKE A LEAF BLOWER...

WHAT I KNOW IS THAT I HAD A CHANCE TO ALLY MYSELF WITH THE MOST POWERFUL WITCH OF HER TIME...
...AND MY TEAM COULDN'T KEEP UP.

AAAH!

GODDESS, THAT WATER IS COLD.

YES. I SEE.
I MEAN I KNOW.
I MEAN A...WHAT?

THEY SAY YOU'RE NO GOOD.

THAT YOU RUN IN CIRCLES, THE SNAKE THAT EATS ITS TAIL.

I'VE GOT A BIT OF A REP MYSELF.

THERE IS NO JOURNEY.
THERE IS JUST WITHIN.
SO MY PATH IS WHERE NONE'S BEATEN...

AND FOR TRUTH, I CHOOSE THE TRICKSTER.

YOU'RE PUTTING YOURSELF IN MY HANDS?
I EXPECT IT WILL COME TO THAT.

I'LL KNOW IF YOU LIE.
I ALWAYS LIE.
THAT'S HOW I'LL KNOW.
SO HOW DO WE START?
finis

COVERS FROM

# BUFFY THE VAMPIRE SLAYER

ISSUES #31 AND #33–#35

By

GEORGES JEANTY

with

DEXTER VINES & MICHELLE MADSEN

DARK HORSE COMICS
SEASON EIGHT
No. 31
$2.99
JOSS WHEDON GEORGES JEANTY
Buffy the vampire slayer™
TURBULENCE
ANDY OWENS
MICHELLE MADSEN
RICHARD STARKINGS
GEORGES 09

*A gag version of the #33 cover revealing Twilight as President Barack Obama.*

GEORGES.
AFTER BENDER
VINES
2009

EXECUTIVE PRODUCER JOSS WHEDON
BRAD MELTZER GEORGES JEANTY
ANDY OWENS MICHELLE MADSEN RICHARD STARKINGS
BUFFY
THE VAMPIRE SLAYER!
TWILIGHT
PART 4

Cover sketches from Jo Chen for *Buffy the Vampire Slayer* covers #32, #34, and #35. Jo always sends a variety of images for the creative team to choose from for the final cover image. Finished art for these covers are on pages 30, 80, and 106.

The following image for *Buffy* #35 features Angel wearing his Twilight mask. This was for solicitation only so as to maintain Twilight's secret identity until readers had the comics.

RIGHT: Final cover from *Willow: Goddesses and Monsters*, by Karl Moline with Andy Owens and Michelle Madsen.

Cover concepts from Moline.

Moline's earliest design of Muffitt and her super-high-tech wheelchair.

Character designs by Moline. Above is Gnog before a fight an after a fight with Willow.

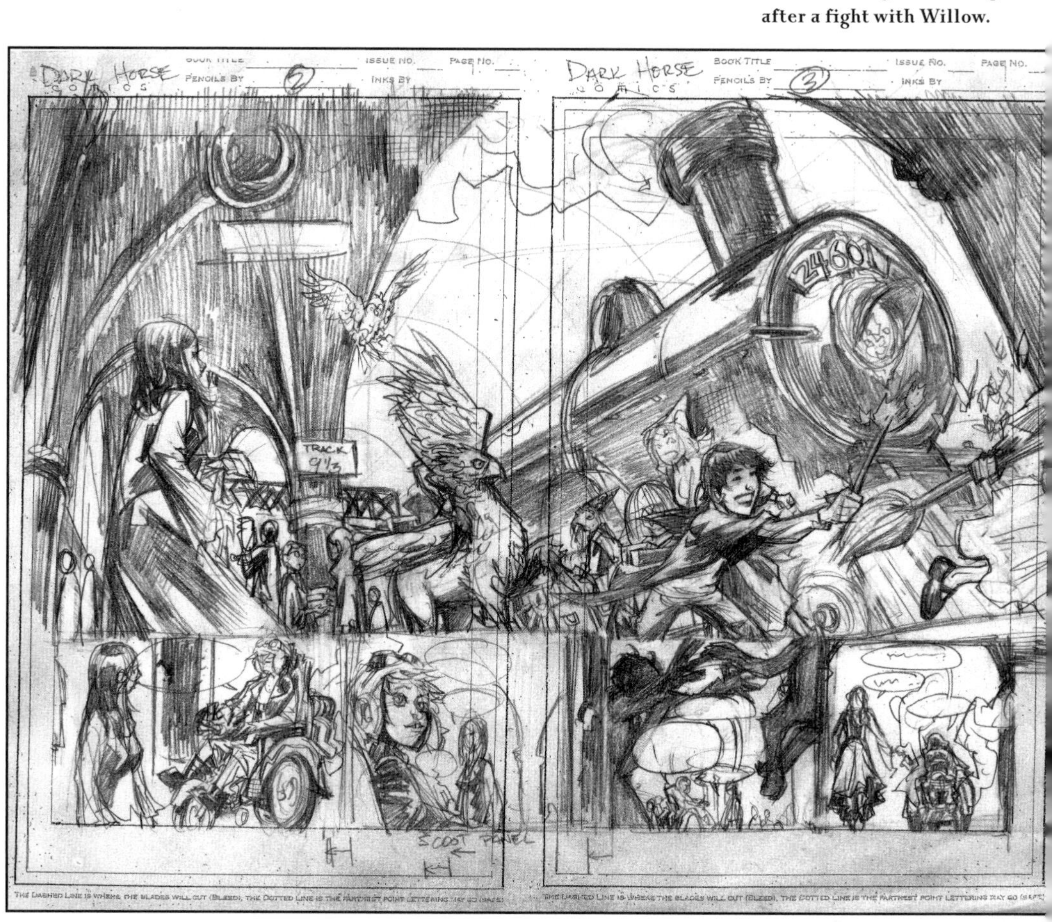


The rough pencils of the Harry Potter-esque sequence.

# RECOMMENDED DARK HORSE READING . . .

**MYSPACE DARK HORSE PRESENTS VOLUMES 1–3**

*Various*

e online comics anthology *MySpace Dark Horse Presents* sees print these three volumes—each collecting six issues of the ongoing se-s. Top talents from the industry like Mike Mignola, Joss Whedon, c Powell, Adam Warren, John Arcudi, and many others bring new sions and stories. They are joined by some of the freshest new lent out there today—found on MySpace! These are premier com-s unlike anything else! *MySpace.com/DarkHorsePresents*

$19.99 EACH

/OLUME 1: ISBN 978-1-59307-998-7 | VOLUME 2: ISBN 978-1-59582-248-2
/OLUME 3: ISBN 978-1-59582-327-4 | VOLUME 4: ISBN 978-1-59582-405-9
VOLUME 5: ISBN 978-1-59582-570-4

**SINFEST VOLUME 1**

*Tatsuya Ishida*

*Sinfest* is one of the most-read and longest-running webcomics out there, and explores religion, advertising, sex, and politics in a way fleen.com calls "both brutally funny and devastatingly on-target." In an era when most syndicated newspaper strips are watered down and uninspired, creator Tatsuya Ishida draws on influences ranging from *Calvin and Hobbes* and *Peanuts* to manga and pop culture to bring us a breath of fresh air.

$14.99 | ISBN 978-1-59582-319-9

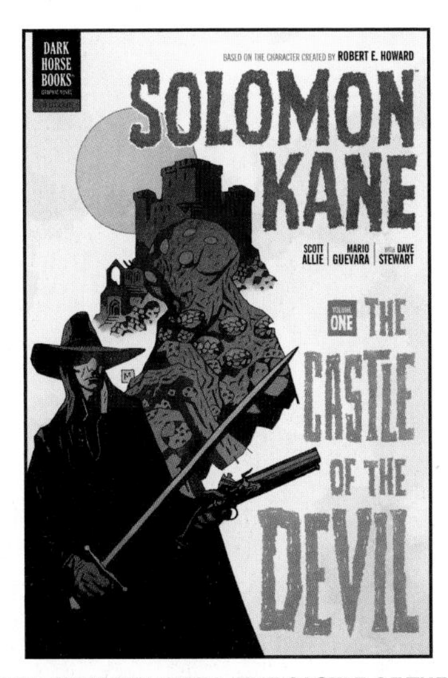


**SOLOMON KANE VOLUME 1: THE CASTLE OF THE DEVIL**

*Scott Allie, Mario Guevara, Dave Stewart, Mike Mignola*

obert E. Howard's vengeance-obsessed puritan begins his super-atural adventures in the haunted Black Forest of Germany in this daptation of Howard's "The Castle of the Devil." When Solomon ane stumbles upon the body of a boy hanged from a rickety allows, he goes after the man responsible—a baron feared by the easants from miles around. Something far worse than the devilish aron or the terrible, intelligent wolf that prowls the woods lies idden in the ruined monastery beneath the baron's castle, where a evil-worshiping priest died in chains centuries ago.

$15.99 | ISBN 978-1-59582-282-6

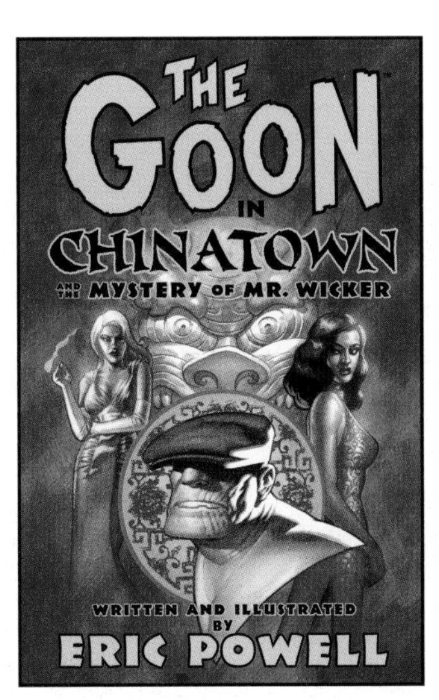


**THE GOON VOLUME 6: CHINATOWN**

*Eric Powell*

Collected in softcover for the very first time, the critically acclaimed *Chinatown* marks Powell's first self-contained graphic novel, which chronicles the misadventures of Goon and his wisecracking side-kick, Franky. When a mysterious new figure enters the crime scene and begins taking out the Goon's business operations one by one, the Goon struggles to keep the city's organized crime under his control as his mind is haunted by the memories of his darkest mo-ment . . . when his mind and body were left scarred . . . and his heart was left black.

$15.99 | ISBN 978-1-59582-406-6

**AVAILABLE AT YOUR LOCAL COMICS SHOP OR BOOKSTORE**

**To find a comics shop in your area, call 1-888-266-4226**

**For more information or to order direct visit darkhorse.com or call 1-800-862-0052**

**Mon.–Fri. 9 AM to 5 PM Pacific Time.**

***Prices and availability subject to change without notice**

**darkhorse.com**

# FROM JOSS WHEDON

## BUFFY THE VAMPIRE SLAYER SEASON 8:

VOLUME 1: THE LONG WAY HOME
*Joss Whedon and Georges Jeanty*
ISBN 978-1-59307-822-5 | $15.99

VOLUME 2: NO FUTURE FOR YOU
*Brian K. Vaughan, Georges Jeanty, and Joss Whedon*
ISBN 978-1-59307-963-5 | $15.99

VOLUME 3: WOLVES AT THE GATE
*Drew Goddard, Georges Jeanty, and Joss Whedon*
ISBN 978-1-59582-165-2 | $15.99

VOLUME 4: TIME OF YOUR LIFE
*Joss Whedon, Jeph Loeb, Georges Jeanty, and others*
ISBN 978-1-59582-310-6 | $15.99

VOLUME 5: PREDATORS AND PREY
*Joss Whedon, Jane Espenson, Cliff Richards, Georges Jeanty, and others*
ISBN 978-1-59582-342-7 | $15.99

VOLUME 6: RETREAT
*Joss Whedon, Jane Espenson, Cliff Richards, Georges Jeanty, and others*
ISBN 978-1-59582-415-8 | $15.99

VOLUME 7: TWILIGHT
*Joss Whedon, Brad Meltzer, and Georges Jeanty*
ISBN 978-1-59582-558-2 | $16.99

TALES OF THE SLAYERS
*Joss Whedon, Amber Benson, Gene Colan, P. Craig Russell, Tim Sale, and others*
ISBN 978-1-56971-605-2 | $14.99

TALES OF THE VAMPIRES
*Joss Whedon, Brett Matthews, Cameron Stewart, and others*
ISBN 978-1-56971-749-3 | $15.99

FRAY: FUTURE SLAYER
*Joss Whedon and Karl Moline*
ISBN 978-1-56971-751-6 | $19.99

SERENITY VOLUME 1: THOSE LEFT BEHIND
*Joss Whedon, Brett Matthews, and Will Conrad*
ISBN 978-1-59307-449-4 | $9.99

SERENITY VOLUME 2: BETTER DAYS
ISBN 978-1-59582-162-1 | $9.99

SERENITY VOLUME 3: THE SHEPHERD'S TALE
ISBN 978-1-59582-561-2 | $14.99

# ALSO FROM DARK HORSE . . .

## BUFFY THE VAMPIRE SLAYER OMNIBUS

VOLUME 1
ISBN 978-1-59307-784-6 | $24.99

VOLUME 2
ISBN 978-1-59307-826-3 | $24.99

VOLUME 3
ISBN 978-1-59307-885-0 | $24.99

VOLUME 4
ISBN 978-1-59307-968-0 | $24.99

VOLUME 5
ISBN 978-1-59582-225-3 | $24.99

VOLUME 6
ISBN 978-1-59582-242-0 | $24.99

VOLUME 7
ISBN 978-1-59582-331-1 | $24.99

BUFFY THE VAMPIRE SLAYER: PANEL TO PANEL
ISBN 978-1-59307-836-2 | $19.99

MYSPACE DARK HORSE PRESENTS VOLUME 1
*Featuring "Sugarshock" by Joss Whedon and Fábio Moon*
ISBN 978-1-59307-998-7 | $17.99

**DARK HORSE BOOKS**®
darkhorse.com



**AVAILABLE AT YOUR LOCAL COMICS SHOP OR BOOKSTO**
To find a comics shop in your area, call 1-888-266-4226.
For more information or to order direct: • On the web: darkhorse.com • E-r
mailorder@darkhorse.com • Phone: 1-800-862-0052
Mon.–Fri. 9 AM to 5 PM Pacific Time.
*Prices and availability subject to change without notice

SEASON EIGHT VOLUME 7

# TWILIGHT

"[*Buffy* Season Eight] continues to evoke the tone and savvy emotional mix of the show."
—The Huffington Post

"Meltzer . . . pulls off an incredible one-two punch, deftly jumping from one emotional high to a drastically different one, leaving readers' heads spinning and me laughing uproariously."
—ComicsAlliance

". . . The true star of this series is Georges Jeanty. He so effectively renders these characters on the page at this point that they emote all of the idiosyncrasies that the television actors themselves established years ago."
—IGN

"Meltzer's take [on *Buffy* Season Eight] definitely has the energy that I would associate with, say, Season Three of the television series, and the art really only gets better."
—Newsarama

"Meltzer's talent speaks for itself. I wouldn't be surprised if letters started pouring in today for him to return for Season Nine."
—Girls Entertainment Network

It's a bird, it's a plane, it's . . . Buffy?

Buffy and the Big Bad of Season Eight, Twilight, reunite in a battle that will take them through time and space, rocking the foundation of civilization—ultimately revealing Twilight's true identity and master plan. Adding to the mayhem is the surprise return of Buffy's first love, Angel.

In this penultimate volume of Season Eight, *New York Times* best-selling author Brad Meltzer (*The Book of Lies*, *Identity Crisis*) joins series artist Georges Jeanty for the groundbreaking arc *Twilight*. This volume also features two stories by series creator and executive producer Joss Whedon.

GRAPHIC NOVEL/ACTION ADVENTURE

DARK HORSE BOOKS

$16.99 U.S.
darkhorse.com

ISBN 978-1-59582-558-2
51699>
9 781595 825582